C000272179

the wishing book

Grahame Howard

PNEUMA SPRINGS PUBLISHING UK

First Published in 2009 by:
Pneuma Springs Publishing

The Wishing Book
Copyright © 2009   Grahame Howard
ISBN: 978-1-905809-64-6

This is a work of fiction. Names, characters, places and incidents are either products of the author's imagination or are used fictitiously. Any resemblance to actual events or locales or persons, living or dead, save those clearly in the public domain, is purely coincidental.

Pneuma Springs Publishing
A Subsidiary of Pneuma Springs Ltd.
7 Groveherst Road, Dartford Kent, DA1 5JD.
E: admin@pneumasprings.co.uk
W: www.pneumasprings.co.uk

A catalogue record for this book is available from the British Library.

Published in the United Kingdom. All rights reserved under International Copyright Law. Contents and/or cover may not be reproduced in whole or in part without the express written consent of the publisher.

the wishing book

Dedicated to my wife Hazel who gave me constant encouragement during the concept and the writing of this book

GLOSSARY

Blattidae A giant cockroach which is Planet Mar's greatest Weapon. This creature will devour anything in its path, including the Martians.

Rogangoes Orange type, ruby coloured berries, found on Planet Mars and ideal for eating.

Troganbugs Small vehicles like a motor bike but without wheels. They are fitted with a sidecar and can transport up to 4 people or Martians.

Antisum A deactivating spray that causes the person that it is fired at to turn into stone for 30 minutes.

Leoxostone A volcanic gemstone that is located in the HQ of Zelmut, the Chief and Highness of the Martians. The Leoxostone has powers to locate things on Earth and Mars and can offer great powers when needed.

Warriors Martians

Termans Large flying bat like creatures that are used for attack purposes.

Olympus Mons This is the highest known mountain in the Solar system. Zelmut's HQ is based within this mountain.

Valles Marineris This is the largest canyon on Mars with a length of 4000km and a depth of 7km.

PROLOGUE

PLANET MARS 1999

Zezmatas was feeling happy with himself as he was transported to Planet Earth. He was well thought of by Zelmut, the Chief and Highness of the Martians on Planet Mars. He had been specially selected and trained to go on a mission to Planet Earth to locate and retrieve the little red wishing book which at the moment was known to be in the hands of the Armaz family on the Island of Tenerife in The Canary Islands.

It had come to the attention of Zelmut that this book had the power to grant wishes to whoever was holding the book. It had been given to a member of the Armaz family, word by word in a dream and his family had been given great wealth.

Zelmut had learned about this from the Leoxostone, a volcanic gemstone in his kingdom, and he wanted the book so that he could fulfil his dream and rule over the whole universe. The Leoxostone had revealed that the book was in the hands of the Armaz family in Los Christianos, in South Tenerife. It was probably at their home but he could not be sure of this. It was Zezmatas' mission to find this book and bring it to Zelmut who would then greatly reward him.

Zezmatas had spent a few weeks observing the vast villa where the Armaz family lived. He didn't want to make any mistakes by rushing things. He had tracked the family to the villa and all he had to do now, was find the book. He could then return home in a blaze of glory.

It was a very warm night as Zezmatas crept round the side of the villa. To anyone who saw him, he looked like a normal Tenerifian. He was heavily suntanned, dressed in a T shirt and shorts and could easily been mistaken for a local. However, he had thought that coming to the villa at night, he would stand a better chance of finding the book, undetected.

Before Zezmatas had left Planet Mars, he had been allowed to stroke the beloved Leoxostone. This experience would help him to overcome difficult situations, like was presented now – a locked window.

Zezmatas stroked the area of the window where the handle was located on the inside. Instantly, the handle melted and he managed to pull it open without any particular problem. This activated the Leoxostone back on Planet Mars and gave it the power to instantly detect and deactivate any burglar alarm or any other system that was installed within the house.

Therefore, he was able to climb through the window with the confidence that there would be no surprises. That is, except if he were to wake any human or animal that may be around. However, he was prepared for this and grasped in his hand a special spray called Antisum that had the ability to temporally freeze anything that tried to attack him, leaving them like a statue. This would only deactivate them for 30 minutes however, so he would need to be quick.

Zezmatas looked around the spacious room he was standing in. It was dark, but his Martian eyes had infrared ability connected to its brain and he was able to see quite clearly.

One thing the Leoxostone couldn't do was to show the exact location of the book. It had the power to show the nearest location within a 5 mile radius but that was all. The actual finding of the book would be down to him.

Quietly, he made his way through the room until he stood before a cabinet.

"Now where would someone hide such a precious thing," he thought.

After trying the cabinet and various drawers and cupboards, he was still no further. He glanced at his watch. It was 3am. He must find it soon and be on his way. He noticed a cupboard that he hadn't opened. It was near the window at the rear of the lounge. With his heart beating ten to the dozen, he pulled the door open and discovered a safe inside.

Ordinarily, a safe this size would deter most burglars. However, Zezmatas, rubbed his hand over the door handle and dial and they both melted. The door clicked open and he noticed to his delight, the little red book on its own in the interior.

"What do you think you're doing?" said a voice behind him.

Zezmatas spun round and came face to face with Pedro Armaz who was pointing a gun at him. In a flash and just before a dog he had not noticed, leapt up at him, he sprayed the Antisum at Pedro Armaz and the dog. The result was amazing. Pedro Armaz just stood there like a statue of solid stone. The dog was more amazing. He had been sprayed while he was in the air leaping to attack Zezmatas. He remained suspended in the air with no apparent sign of life.

Zezmatas knew that he had no time to waste. He put the small book into his pocket and amazed that no one else had been woken by the noise, he made his way out of the villa and into the warm night air.

Zezmatas made it up to a quiet spot on the beach near Playa de las Americas and sat down to consider his options. The sun was coming up now and glancing at his watch, he noticed that it was 5am.

"Let's have a look at this little prize," he said to himself.

He drew the book from his shorts pocket and skimmed through it. It meant very little to him but he could feel quite an awesome feeling as he held it in the palm of his hand.

"They say that anyone who wishes for something while holding the book will have the wish granted," he thought.

"Well, let's try this out," he said. "I wish that I could be in Australia – Melbourne."

There was a sudden darkness and Zezmatas felt his vision changing as he saw flashes of brilliant colour before his eyes. With one almighty mixing of the colour, reality returned and he found himself, still on a beach but in a much different environment. Zezmatas stood up to view the scenery. As he turned away from the beach, in the distance he could see skyscrapers and very tall towers.

"This is obviously Melbourne" he said, walking in the direction of the City. "I think that I can afford to enjoy myself a little bit before I return home."

And enjoy himself he did. He spent over a month in Australia, visiting different locations, all with the help of the little red book. No pleasure eluded him and he began to like this very different lifestyle. After a while he wished himself to London, England and then down to a County called Dorset.

Zezmatas was enjoying himself so much that he lost track of time. Before he knew it, he had been gone almost 3 years.

Zezmatas failed to realise that a Martian's lifespan on Planet Earth was much different to the eternal life that they enjoyed on Planet Mars. Most were lucky to live past 3 years.

As time went on, he continued to use the little red book to fulfil his every whim. He was actually amazed that Zelmut had not sent anyone to find out why he had taken so much time in obtaining the prize.

"He must really trust me," he thought, laughing to himself.

As time went on he began to feel quite worn out and slowly began to deteriorate until he could hardly walk. He had been living in a most beautiful house set on the coast in Dorset. However, not even wishing on the book changed his state of health and on one particular rainy day, he found himself on a building site. The place was deserted, probably because of the inclement weather.

Zezmatas knew he was dying. His strength was being sucked away from him very rapidly. He had thought about wishing that he could return to Planet Mars but somehow, he had no strength to perform the task and he also didn't want to face the wrath of Zelmut.

He found himself in a building that was being electrically wired. He was upstairs and noticed that there were some floorboards that still had to be nailed down. One of the boards was very small, no longer than a foot in length. He placed the book in the dark crevice and replaced the board hammering it down with a hammer that he found lying close by.

Using every bit of strength that he could summon up, he made his way down the bare wooden stairs and went out into the cool rain. He managed to walk a little way down the lane and then collapsed in some bushes. He gasped for breath as he lay in the cold wet grass.

"My life is over," he gasped. "I have been a fool. I could have had treasures that no one could imagine but I have thrown it all away. Now I must die."

With that, he rolled sideways, died and then disappeared from sight. For Zezmatas, it was all over.

One

*L*ittle John Carter sat in his bedroom. He was bored because it was raining outside. In fact it was a heavy storm and this meant that he had to stay indoors making him feel frustrated because he had nothing to do.

He had been on his computer and this had lasted for about 10 minutes. Now he was playing on his Xbox and despite being an accomplished operator, he just didn't have the staying power to remain focused on winning his way to the next level.

"Life's so boring at times," he thought.

He left the Xbox game feeling he would try again later. He glanced out of the window checking the weather for what must have been the umpteenth time in the last five minutes. It was still raining, in fact it was now pelting it down which only added to his misery.

He got down on his hands and knees to check under his bed to see if there were any games he could play. He spotted a fifty pence coin, something he had dropped and been unable to find about a month ago. It was tucked up in the corner near the skirting board.

As he grabbed it, he pulled up a part of the carpet that had worn away from the floor runners. He was just about to roll the carpet back in place when he noticed that one of the floorboards – a very small piece about a foot long, was wobbly.

On closer inspection, he found that he could easily lift it away from the rest. What he saw as he moved the board away made him gasp! Lying in the small dusty crevice was a little red book covered in dust and cobwebs.

"Cor it's a book," he exclaimed loudly, putting his hand into the hole and removing it.

"I wonder who put this in here."

John wiped the little red book on his shirt and held it for a few moments as if he was holding a bar of gold. Something about it gave him a strange, warm and glowing feeling like he had never known before.

He blew the remaining pieces of dust from the gilt edged pages and opened it. He began to flick through the small pages which had been beautifully handwritten in English. The main content of the book was made up of 5 words: peace, love, happiness, joy and life.

These words were on every page from page 10 through to the final 50th page. Repeated over and over were the phrases:

Peace is yours
Love is yours
Happiness is yours
Joy is yours
Life is yours

"It just goes over and over repeating these words," thought John surprised, "but why?"

John turned to the beginning of the book and thumbed through the first few pages. On page 3 he read:

"I am writing these words from a dream that I had when I was a child.
I grew up on the on the Island of Tenerife in the Canary Islands. My family were very poor and my father used to collect bananas from

the trees there and transport them on camels to the main part of the Island just to make a little money.

We lived in a remote cottage not far from Palo Blanco which is under the shadows of Mount Teide. The mountain is actually the largest of the volcanoes that stand on The Canary Islands and is 12225 feet in height.

It was a very bleak place to live, often very cold, especially in winter when the snow would cover Mount Teide and the surrounding parts. The open spaces leading to the sunny coast, often made me feel that we were living on the moon.

Because of the lack of money and the sheer hard work my parents had to carry out to make ends meet, I began to pray to anyone who would listen, that I could have a wish granted. My wish was for us to be a prosperous family, living in a more relaxed part of the Island.

One night in a dream, the words of this book came to me and I felt compelled to write them down. As I did, I felt the certainty that things would change for the better. They did, quite swiftly. We are now a prosperous family living in peace in Los Christianos which is in the south of the Island.

It is my intention that this book remain in my family's possession eternally. However, if you are reading this, my desire has not been fulfilled. I ask one thing – use it wisely. The words are life-changing. Whenever you make a wish, touch the book and your wish will be granted. The book must always be touched by the person making the wish for it to be fulfilled. Without the book, nothing will happen.

My one request is, when you have finished with this book – hence happy and prosperous, that it is returned to my family at Los Christianos, Tenerife."

Pedro Armaz
1940

Two

*J*ohn, who was nine years old, read the note from Pedro Armaz over and over again. His freckled face, showed utter surprise. He couldn't understand how it could have been under his floorboards.

The family had lived in the house for just over 4 years, moving to Dorset from the Midlands so that his dad could find a suitable job. It wasn't a new house, perhaps 10 years old.

"Perhaps the previous tenants had put it there or perhaps the builders, but why?" he said. "Also it was written so long ago, 1940. That's 69 years ago. How did it find its way into our house?"

Outside the rain was still falling out of the sky but now John had a new lease of life. The words of the book excited him and he couldn't wait to try it out. However, what could he wish for? Ordinarily he would have had several things that he would like to happen, but now, faced with the opportunity, his mind couldn't come up with anything particularly tangible. He considered wishing that it would stop raining but decided that was not exciting enough.

"I'll do that later," he thought. "Now what else can I do?"

Just then, it came to him.

"I know," he said, "I'll wish that I was a fly. At least I'll find out if it works, and as long as I can touch the book, I can turn back again."

And that's what he did. He stood up with the little red book in his hand as if he were taking an oath in court.

"I wish that I was a fly," he said.

Just then, everything seemed to go chaotic. The place went very dark and then vivid colours began to come into his vision – purple, pink, orange and red. This was followed by a burst of the colours mixed up, rather like a firework display.

All of a sudden the vision of colour had gone and the light returned. He suddenly realised with a mixture of excitement and extreme apprehension that he was sitting on top of the little red book which was resting on his dressing table. He was a fly.

He didn't feel any different at all. In fact, he felt that he had all of his faculties. He just felt strange. He realised that he had no hands or feet, not like he had before. He was total fly.

"I don't know if I like this," he thought as he sat there feeling vulnerable, "but I suppose I'd better give it a go."

With that, he launched himself off the book and landed on the wall behind the dresser.

"Wow, I can fly," he said feeling elated with this new experience. "It's strange though looking up the wall. I keep thinking that I'm going to fall off, and I feel dizzy."

The door of his bedroom was open slightly so he flew cautiously through the 12 inch gap and headed down the stairs. He would have liked to have gone into Penny's room. Penny was John's twin sister. However, her door was closed.

Disappointed, he flew into the hall and then straight into the kitchen where his parents were sitting at a table drinking a cup of tea.

"I hope this rain is not here for the weekend," his dad said, "I wanted to clean the car."

"Well I suppose it's getting cleaned with all of this water," replied John's mum.

"Yes, but it's not the same," replied his dad.

John landed on the wall next to where his dad was sitting.

"Hey dad; mum." he shouted, "Look it's me."

Of course, no words could be heard from John, except the buzzing sound that flies make.

"What's that fly doing in here?" shouted his dad trying to swot it with his newspaper.

"No dad, don't," shouted John in panic, "you'll kill me. It's me, John."

All this resulted in more buzzing and John's dad got up from his chair and opened a door under the sink. He brought out a can of fly spray.

"No dad," John screamed. "You'll kill me if you squirt it at me."

John managed to make it through the kitchen door and up the stairs before his dad had realised the fly had gone. With panic and his heart pounding, he landed on the little red book.

"I don't want to be a fly," he shouted. "I want to be me. I wish to be changed back to the way I was."

The room once again went dark and the vivid pattern of colour returned culminating into the burst of firework display.

John was still shouting when he realised that he had been changed back into himself. The wish had come true – twice.

"This is amazing," he said. "Mind you, I don't ever want to be a fly again. I thought I was a goner when dad got the fly spray out."

"Why are you shouting?" asked his dad, coming into John's bedroom with the fly spray still in his hand.

"I wasn't," John replied.

"Yes you were," his dad said, "You were shouting, 'I don't want to be a fly.' What's it all about?"

"Oh that," said John thinking on his feet. "I was just singing a new rap song that I heard on the radio earlier."

"Funny you should say that, I tried to swot a fly downstairs just now, anyway that's a strange song if you ask me," replied his dad turning to go out of the room, "By the way, your lunch will be ready soon." And with that he was gone.

"Cor that was close," thought John. "I'll have to be more careful in future."

He was still a little shaky from his near-death experience as a fly but he was also elated that the little red book had worked.

He thought again about wishing that it would stop raining, but decided that he'd had enough for the moment. Instead, he decided to head downstairs for his lunch.

"It's going to be awesome," he said as he went down.

Three

*J*ohn had slept long and hard since he had found the little red book. He had not used the book again since he found it the previous day following his experiment as a fly. Such was his shock at his experience that he had decided to give it a break until he was alone with his sister Penny. This happened later in the day when they were playing in her room.

They decided that they would play Pinball on John's laptop. John was an expert and Penny came in pretty close. However, after John had been to the bathroom to wish that he would get the highest score ever, she wouldn't play it anymore favouring Monopoly.

Again, following John wishing that he would clear the board of all the property and the money, she begun to sulk and say that he was, "a horrid little boy."

"Come on Penny," he said, "let's play just one more time. You may win this time."

"I'm not playing with you at all, ever," she said pouting and shaking her head so that her short pony tail shook from side to side.

"Then I'm not going to tell you my secret," he said, and walked back into his own bedroom.

There was a pause of about two minutes before Penny knocked on John's door and walked in.

"What secret?" she asked inquisitively.

"I'm not telling you" he teased.

"Oh come on John," she pleaded. "I'm sorry for calling you a horrid little boy. I was just upset that you won everything."

"Well, I don't know," said John, "I'm not so sure that you would keep it a secret."

"I would, I promise," she said pleading with him again. "Please John."

Oh okay," he said. "Come and sit down, it's a long story."

John then went on to tell her about finding the book and what had happened to him. She listened intently until he had finished.

"That's poppycock," she laughed, "that could never happen, you're winding me up."

"It's true Penny," John said, feeling quite hurt that his sister disbelieved him and was laughing at him in such a manner.

"Prove it then," she challenged, "turn yourself back into a fly."

"No way," John said, "I've had enough of flies to last a life time."

"Well turn yourself into a monkey then," Penny continued, "that's if you can, which I doubt."

"That might be tricky," said John, "if dad comes into the bedroom and catches me like that, he may telephone the RSPCA or something and have me taken away before I can change back. I know though, what about wishing that mum brings us up some lovely cream cakes and ice cream?"

"She never does that," said Penny, you know what she's like about us eating in our bedrooms."

"I know," said John, "so that would convince you wouldn't it?"

"It might," she said, "but?"

"I tell you what," continued John, "I'll wish for the cakes and ice cream and then when we've ate them, we'll go out and do something a little more daring. What do you say?"

"Okay, that's a deal," Penny said.

*J*ohn sat on his bed and picked up the little red book. Penny looked at him as if he had turned into a mad person as he began to make a wish that their mum would come up the stairs within a few minutes with delicious cream cakes and ice cream.

John again experienced the darkening of the room followed by the brilliant flashes of colour before it all ended with the firework display at the end.

As John opened his eyes and focused on his sister, suddenly there was a tap at his door and their mum walked in with a tray. She put it down on the bedside cabinet and looked at them.

"I thought you deserved a treat," she said, "the weather was awful yesterday and you had to stay in. So I decided to get you these. Come on, don't look so shocked. Tuck into them." With that she left the room.

Penny was absolutely amazed and just kept staring at the delights that their mum had just placed on John's cabinet. It took her a full minute to realise that John was tucking into the feast like he hadn't eaten for a month.

"I, I don't believe it," she stammered, "I just don't believe that this has happened."

"I told you didn't I?" answered John with a mouthful of cake," let's scoff this lot down and then we'll go out and you will see what we can really do."

*I*t was about 4pm when they made their way out onto the street. They had decided that they would go across the fields that were facing the house and see what they could find to wish for. They had been told that they were not to go too far. Across the fields would be okay as long as they didn't wander too far away from the house.

They came to a big old oak tree that must have been there for years, it was so high that John and Penny could not see the top of it very clearly. John and his friend Jimmy had often planned one day to try and climb it. However, up to now, they had only made the first branch which was about 9 feet off the ground.

John decided that he could wish for that now. He had always wanted to do it so why not give it a go? He mentioned this to Penny, enquiring if she would like to go up there with him. However she declined.

"You've got to be joking," she said. "Wild horses wouldn't get me up there."

"They would if I wished for them," John said jokingly.

"Don't you dare John Carter," she screamed. "I'd never talk to you again."

"Well if I wish to go up the tree on my own, you won't be able to see that I'm up there," John said quite concerned.

"You could always wish that the tree could vanish," said Penny.

"Wow, that's a great idea," said John becoming excited, "come on, let's do it."

John picked up the book and began to speak quietly, in fact so quietly that Penny could hardly hear him.

"I wish that this old oak tree vanishes without any sign that it has ever been here," he whispered.

Once again, John went through the strange colour features in his head and within a few moments, the tree had disappeared.

"I can't believe it," shouted Penny. "This is absolutely awesome. Wait till I tell my friends at school tomorrow."

"You can't do that," said John.

"Why can't I?" Penny replied beginning to pout again.

"It's obvious," replied John. "We've got to be careful who we tell or everyone will want to see the book and we could end up losing it."

"Are you going to tell anyone?" she asked.

"Only Jimmy," he replied... "He won't tell anyone."

"That's not fair," Penny cried. "I want to tell Jackie. If it's all right for you, then it's okay for me."

"No don't do that," said John appalled. "Can't you remember last year when you fell out with her, she told everyone that you fancied Johnny Taylor? No, Jimmy's your friend as well and I suggest that he is the only one we tell. Do you agree?"

"Okay," she said. What about the tree, are you going to put it back?"

"I'm tempted to leave it over night to see what happens," said John. "Can you imagine people's faces when they notice that it's missing?"

"They probably wouldn't notice," Penny replied, "but it's a great idea. Let's leave it until after school tomorrow."

Four

Zelmut sat on his throne high up in the region of Olympus Mons, the highest mountain on the face of Planet Mars. He was the Chief of the Martians and ruled with a rod of iron. Everyone on the planet feared him and this made him feel very superior.

He had been considering what was happening on Planet Earth. Back in 1999, a well trained and highly respected warrior by the name of Zezmatas had received the highest honour that Planet Mars could bestow upon a Martian. He had been specially selected and trained to go to Planet Earth to find and bring back the little red book to his chief. For this, he would receive the highest honour of being second in charge of the Martian warriors. This was an honour that Martians could only dream about.

Zelmut had heard about the powers of this little red book and how it had changed the life of the humans who were in possession of it, and wanted it for himself. With it in his possession, he could rule the whole of the Solar system, the whole of the universe.

However, Zezmatas had betrayed him and the whole of Planet Mars. Instead of stealing this prize from the Armaz family and taking it to Zelmut, he had used it for himself - for his own selfish gain. He had stolen the book in Tenerife and had travelled halfway around Planet Earth finally settling in a place called England where he used the power of this book for his own pleasures.

Zezmatas though, had failed to remember that, while on Planet Mars, the Martians life span was eternal, unless they were unfortunate enough to be hit by a vaporising gun, which would cause them to melt completely. However, once a Martian had left the atmosphere of the Planet and travelled to Planet Earth, their life span then became mortal, in fact they only existed for about 3 years.

Zelmut had heard that Zezmatas had died on Planet Earth and had hidden the little red book, possibly in a house or other type of building. This is all that he knew at the time.

Now, through the power of the Leoxostone – a volcanic gemstone that had powers to detect other such forceful powers throughout the universe, he had been informed that the little red book was once again being used in England.

With close counsel from his trusty Martian assistant, Yermin, he discovered that there was once again a mighty warrior who was named Taneka, who would be able to fulfil Zelmut's dream of power.

Taneka had been selected and briefed very clearly about what his mission would be. He was to travel to Planet Earth and bring back this most coveted and treasured gift to Zelmut who would reward him handsomely.

With this settled, Taneka made his trip through the vast Solar system to fulfil his mission for his master.

"Right children," said the teacher, Mr Jackson, putting his glasses on the top of his head," listen in and be quiet when I tell you to. We are going to be looking at the life of the well known author and poet, Thomas Hardy. I want you to take your exercise books out and write down a short piece, perhaps a paragraph, on what you know about him. Okay, you can begin."

"Who did he say?" whispered John to his best friend, Jimmy.

"Thomas Hardy," replied Jimmy, "although I didn't think he was a writer. I thought he was Lord Nelson's right hand man."

"Lord who," asked Penny, who was sitting nearby.

"You know," said John, "the bloke who sailed on that flagship."

"It was Thomas Masterman Hardy, to be precise," added Jimmy, who always felt that he was an authority on most things.

The children were pupils at The John Williams Primary School in a village in Dorset, It wasn't a bad school as far as schools go, However, the children had different opinions about this and couldn't wait to move on to the Secondary School up the road.

The children wrote a brief paragraph about this chap and handed them in to the teacher.

"Okay," said Mr Jackson, "I can see from your notes that no one in particular has even heard of Hardy. However, three of you have obviously been copying or conferring with each other. Jimmy Swift and John and Penny Carter, I will see you after this lesson. You obviously do not know the difference between an eminent writer and a naval officer."

"Oh flipping heck, that's not fair," whispered John. "I thought you knew about such things Jimmy? I regret not wishing for the right answer now."

Jimmy remained quiet. He had been certain that he had got the right chap. He thought he would challenge Mr Jackson about it later.

Meanwhile, John was a little irritated that they had suffered such injustice and he thought he would teach the high and mighty Mr Jackson a lesson himself. He clutched the little red book and quietly wished that all of Mr Jackson's writing would disappear from the chalkboard.

Once again the familiar darkness came all around him and the colours that John by now, was becoming accustomed to. Suddenly, all of the writing had vanished.

Mr Jackson obviously unaware of what had happened, was totally flabbergasted that the notes that had taken him a considerable time to write, were now not on the board.

"What on earth?" he spluttered as he looked at the board with his mouth agape. "This is preposterous," he continued. "Where on earth are my notes?"

John and Penny, who were the only people who knew what had happened, were in a fit of the giggles.

"Quiet," shouted Mr Jackson, still totally bewildered by what had happened to him. "I will have no giggling in my lesson. Now each of you, write 100 times, 'we will not laugh during a lesson.'"

As Mr Jackson frantically searched through his desk drawer for his notes, John once again took the book in his hand and wished that the chalkboard writing of Mr Jackson's would reappear. After a few moments, it did.

It took a few moments for Mr Jackson to take control of himself. Once he was assured that he was, he returned to the chalkboard preparing to write the account again. He was astounded that he could now plainly see his notes on the board. He sat down without a comment and stared into space for what seemed like ages.

After a while, he said.

"Okay class dismissed, I have an important meeting to attend. Go to the library and swot up on Thomas Hardy the writer, until your next lesson.

With that he walked out of the classroom and went home.

"What happened?" asked Jimmy as they walked out of the school to make their way home. "How did the writing vanish off the board and then come back again?"

Jimmy had been John's friend from the day that John's family had moved into their house some 4 years ago. They had been inseparable since that day and latterly, Penny, who was a tomboy, had joined in the friendship.

They continued down the road for a little while until they came to the fields which once had an old oak tree. Crowds had gathered there, totally perplexed that there was no sign that a tree had ever been there.

"What's happening over there?" Jimmy asked, walking across to the fields. "Flipping heck, someone's taken the tree down. We'll never be able to climb up there now."

"I think it's time to have a chat," said John, winking at his sister who was also walking with them. "I tell you what, let's all go home and get changed and we'll meet back at the fields. I've got something really fantastic to tell you."

Jimmy, who lived 3 doors away from John and Penny's house, sauntered off home with the promise that they would meet up over the fields in 30 minutes.

*T*he place was buzzing when John and Penny walked in their house. Mum was watching the news on television and hoping for an explanation to how a massive oak tree could vanish into thin air.

"Hi mum," John said, "what's happening over the fields?"

"I'd have thought that you would have heard," his mum replied. "The old oak tree has gone missing."

"Missing?" said Penny, "How can a tree go missing?"

"People noticed that it wasn't there this morning," their mum continued, "it's been all over the news. It's just vanished without a trace and what's more, there's no sign that it had ever been there in the first place. It's incredible. The news is intimating that it could be the work of aliens."

"Aliens?" asked John, "What do you mean, Martians or something?"

"That's what they're saying," replied their mum.

"Flipping heck," said Penny, "we'll get changed and go and have a look."

"Make sure you don't go any further than there though," said their mum, "and tea will be ready at 5.30, so you've only got a couple of hours."

*J*ohn, Penny and Jimmy met up shortly after 3.30 pm. They avoided the crowd that had been there for most of the day and sat down on a small hill where they had a perfect view of the empty space that had once been a tree.

"What have you got to tell me then?" asked Jimmy eagerly. He knew it was something exciting and he couldn't wait any longer.

John and Penny explained in graphic detail what had been happening over the last twenty-four hours. They left nothing out, even explaining how Mr Jackson's chalkboard had been targeted. After about thirty minutes, John had fully explained everything to Jimmy and began to show him the little red book.

"I don' believe you," Jimmy said, "you're winding me up."

"It's true Jimmy," said Penny. "I didn't believe it at first until John had wished for the cakes and then the oak tree vanishing. You can't deny that."

"My dad said it was the work of some Martians," said Jimmy. "They came in the night, some people saw them."

"Well the writing vanishing off Jackson's board wasn't the work of Martians was it?" said John defensively. "How do you explain that?"

"I can't," Jimmy said.

"Look I'll prove it to you," said John, "but you've got to promise on the bible that you won't tell a soul about it. Okay?"

"Okay," replied Jimmy, "I promise. Put the tree back and I'll believe you."

"I can't do that at this moment can I?" said John, "there's dozens of people around. It'll have to be done during the night or something, when there's no one about."

"That'll take ages," said Jimmy, "People are planning to camp out to see if the Martians will return."

John sighed at this news. He had planned to wish the tree back when it got dark. It now looked like he would have to wait ages to be able to do this without anyone actually seeing it being replaced. He had considered wishing the tree back while the crowd was there. However, he wasn't too sure that people would be safe.

"What if the tree crushed somebody while it was being replaced?" he had thought." That would be awful. No, he felt the safest way was at night time, even if he had to wait for weeks.

"*I* tell you what," said Jimmy, "wish that someone dressed up as Micky Mouse drives up right now to look at the tree. I'll believe you then."

"Okay," said John, taking the book out of his pocket. "I'll do just that."

John stood up with the book in his hand. The others stood in front of him so that the crowd couldn't see what he was doing. With total confidence, he began to speak.

"I wish that someone dressed as Micky Mouse will drive up to this field right now to have a look at what has happened to the tree."

Even though the other two children couldn't see what was happening, John felt it go dark once again and the familiar pattern of colours began to cascade before his eyes. Within a few moments, it was all over and they all looked around to see what had happened.

After a few minutes, Micky Mouse still had not turned up and Jimmy was beginning to become even more sceptical than he had originally been.

"I told you it was a load of old bunkum," he said to John and Penny. "You've been winding me up all the time.

With that, a pale blue sports car drove up the track to where they were sitting. Inside the car was someone dressed in a Micky Mouse outfit? He pulled up in the car and wound the window down as if he was going to ask them something. However, at the last moment, he changed his mind and continued to sit in the car.

No one had noticed that such a celebrity had turned up. Such was the excitement that Micky Mouse went unnoticed. He continued to sit in the car for a few moments and finally, changing his mind, wound the window down to speak to the children.

"What's going on kids?" he asked. "Have I missed the action?"

"Cor," was all that Jimmy could manage as he stared at this colourful character speaking with them.

"I was just passing the area," he continued, "when I saw this great crowd. Is something going to happen?"

Penny explained to the large cuddly character what had been happening and he remained for a few minutes before he re-started his car.

"I hope you get your tree back," he shouted as he turned the car around and sped off back down the track."

"I'm in a dream," Jimmy said, "I've just seen Micky Mouse. Am I alive or am I dreaming or what?"

"No," replied John laughing. "You're in a wish and it's the wish that you asked for. Now do you believe us?"

"Wow," said Jimmy, "yes I believe you. That was awesome. I wonder if he was the real Mickey Mouse."

Five

Zelmut paced around his large headquarters that resembled a spaceship more than it did a building. All around were computers and large wall monitors all displaying different views of Planet Mars and the rest of the Solar system. The windows of the building were massive displaying breathtaking view of volcanoes, mountains and the red dusted ground of the planet.

At each computer sat one of Zelmut's highly trained and trusted technical warriors, who continually read data from the screens and tapped in different codes. The warriors were very strange looking. Their height was about 4 foot and they had broad shoulders and a slight hump on their backs. The most characteristic part of their body though, was their heads. They were very small, about half the size of the average human's head. Their faces looked very rough and scarred and they had slanting eyes that gave the impression that they were asleep. Their skin colouring was grey. Their hands and feet were very much like a human's but the fingers were much more tapered at the tips almost to a point.

Zelmut was different. He was much taller, probably 5 feet. His shoulders were broad like the rest but his head appeared much bigger. On closer inspection, this was probably because he wore a triangular maroon coloured helmet that covered the biggest part of his face. All of them wore shiny, maroon all in one suits, with boots that came up to their knees.

In the middle of the room in a breathtaking display, was the Leoxostone, a large volcanic gemstone that had flashing, alternating colours of green, purple, red and orange. The Leoxostone was dark in colour and very shiny. It stood almost 6 feet tall and as the colours changed on a regular basis, a steam like presence could be seen coming from the stone. This was one of Zelmut's prized possessions. It had the power to detect other powerful forces for miles around – even to earth and could ascertain the location within a few miles radius. This was how Zelmut had been able to trace the little red book. However, it could only detect the book when it was in use.

Zelmut's heels clipped on the stone tiles that were made from local rock and trimmed to a smooth finish. He walked back and forth waiting for Yermin his trusty assistant to come from his quarters. He didn't have long to wait.

"Is Taneka in place on Planet Earth?" he asked.

"He is in place your Highness," replied Yermin.

"Then we wait for further news," said Zelmut.

Since Jimmy had realised the truth about the little red book, he had felt a great excitement about all it could achieve for the children.

"We could wish for anything we want," he said to John and Penny as they sat in his bedroom the following Friday night.

"Yes, you're right," said John, "but we've got to be careful. If we get new computers and games and everything else we'd like, our parents would become suspicious."

"Couldn't we wish that they wouldn't notice?" asked Jimmy.

"Someone would notice that's for sure," said Penny, who was always the sensible one.

"That's right," said John, "and we don't want to become greedy by asking for everything we would like. There'll be time for things like that later, but for now, I want us to wish for something absolutely tremendous."

"What are we going to wish for then?" Jimmy asked.

"I fancy Mars," said John.

"What the chocolate bar?" asked Penny laughing loudly.

"Ha, ha," replied John, "very funny. No I mean the planet. It would be fantastic."

"Wow, not half," said Jimmy. "Yea, let's go there."

"What would we say to our parents and school?" asked Penny. "I mean, they'd notice that we're missing wouldn't they? Then they'd contact the police."

"Well, that's true," said John. "It would have to be thought out properly. We could wish that no one would miss us but it's tricky. Let's give it some thought and in the meantime, we can have some fun with it."

"What about the tree?" asked Penny. "Are we going to put it back yet?"

"I was thinking about that," said John. "I don't think there are any people hanging around the field anymore. We could do it tonight. We don't have to be there do we?"

"No that's right," said Jimmy, "but it would be awesome to see, wouldn't it?"

*I*t was 9pm when John and Penny left Jimmy's house. They had decided that they would wait until it was really late and their parents were in bed. They would then go across the field and wish the tree back.

"Let's put our mobiles on to vibrate only," said John. "Then when our parents are asleep we can text each other and set the time to meet up.

With that arranged, John and Penny went home and watched a little television before their parents told them that it was time for bed.

It was 12.30am before John could be sure that his parents were sleeping. They had stayed up to watch the late night film and John and Penny had almost given up hope that they'd ever go to bed. In fact, John had been considering wishing that they would turn in just before he heard them close their bedroom door. Jimmy had texted twice to let them know that his parents had gone to bed. He had texted once at 11pm and then again to see if they were nearly ready at midnight. Finally they were ready and texted Jimmy to meet them.

It was a cold night to say it was June. There was a slight breeze that tended to cut through them as they all made their way to where the tree had once stood. As they neared the location, they stopped to check that there were no people on Martian watch. They satisfied themselves that no other person was visible but were concerned that if people were on watch, they would hardly show themselves. They would be in hiding.

With this in mind, they walked around the perimeter of the field and then slightly into the field until they were satisfied that no one had seen them and that they would have a good view of what was about to happen.

They sat down in the long grass. It was quite damp with the night's dew and this added to their feeling colder. John was just going to get his book out when they heard a rushing sound through the grass that made them freeze with fear.

"What is it?" whispered Penny, feeling very scared.

"I don't know," said John, "but I don't like it.

Jimmy remained quiet. He didn't want the others to realise that he was scared out of his wits.

Suddenly there was a mighty rushing sound of feet running through the grass. Then with an awesome roar, a stag ran by them, so close that they could have touched it.

"**AAARGH,**" screamed Penny at the top of her voice.

Jimmy, hearing the sound and then Penny's piecing shriek, ran towards the edge of the field. John just laid there paralysed with fear.

It seemed ages before anyone spoke. John broke the silence.

"Are you okay Penny?" John finally asked feebly.

"I think so," she replied.

"Where's Jimmy?" John asked.

"I don't know," she said, "the last I saw of him, he was running somewhere."

"I'm here," said Jimmy, "gingerly creeping up to where his friends sat. "What on earth was that?"

"A flipping stag," said John. "It scared me to death. I've never seen one so close before."

"No me neither," said Jimmy, still shaking.

*I*t took the children a good 30 minutes before they were able to proceed. Such was the shock that they had suffered that they had contemplated giving it up and returning home to their beds.

Their eyes were everywhere as they proceeded towards where the old oak tree had been. With every step, they dreaded coming into contact with the stag again.

"Right, this will be far enough," said John, looking around him to satisfy himself that nothing was about. "Let's get the tree back and get back home."

John took his book out and was just about to make the wish when out of the corner of his eye, he saw a man, shrouded in the darkness, staring at them.

"What are you kids up to at this hour?" the man asked them.

With that, John started to run, quickly followed by the others. They didn't stop until they were safely outside their home.

"Is he following us?" asked Penny petrified.

"I can't see him," said John, "flipping heck, I don't know what scared me the most, the stag or him."

"Who was it?" asked Jimmy, "Did anyone get a look at him?"

"I was too busy running," replied Penny, still trying to get her breath back from the exertion.

"Well that's the end of that," said John.

"We can still do it," said Jimmy. "We can make the wish from here."

"I don't know," replied John feeling quite apprehensive.

"Shush," said Penny suddenly spotting the man on the opposite side of their road. He's over there."

With that, they all shot into the shadows of a hedge and peered over at the man who was walking up the street just over from where they were. Every now and then, he would stop as if he was looking for something.

"He's looking for us," said Penny, stifling a scream.

"Hold on," said John, "he's got a dog with him. That's why he keeps stopping."

They continued to stare over at the man. Suddenly a little dog, no bigger than a rabbit, came running up to him.

"Come on Patch," the man said, "we need to get home. It looks like we'll see no Martians tonight. Mind you, I thought those kids were Martians at first. They gave me the fright of my life."

With that, he walked up the road on his way to his home.

"He was just as scared of us," said John, feeling more relieved now. "Boy that was scary. Come on, let's wish that tree back.

*T*he children watched from the safety of their hiding place as the great old oak tree came down from the sky like a giant rocket ship descending from its flight to the moon. The colouring was rather like lightening but with no particular sound, just flashes of purple, gold, scarlet and green. It was over in just a few moments and the old oak tree once again stood tall and proud in the field.

"That was amazing," said Jimmy hardly able to contain himself. "I've never seen anything like it."

"Spectacular," Penny said.

"It was awesome," said John, "but we are not to breathe a word of how the tree got back here, are we in agreement?"

They all agreed and turned to go back to their respective homes in a jubilant mood.

Six

'It is incredibly astonishing that the old oak tree has returned,' said the reporter of the local television news. 'Some people are reporting that it is an Act of God that the Almighty is trying to tell us something. Others favour the popular opinion that aliens, possibly Martians, have landed on the earth and are playing pranks on us. Whatever the answer is, it has sure stirred up a fracas that is spreading around the world fast. Experts are flying into England from all parts of the globe to give us their educated opinions of what may have happened in this tiny Dorset Village.

'One witness told our reporter on the scene that he saw some people that he first thought were children. Let's go over to Dorset live to hear what he has to say.'

"It was about 1am," the man began, "I was walking the dog. I hadn't been able to sleep much since the tree vanished, so I decided to take the dog and see what was about. I was flabbergasted. There were three of them. I thought at first that they were kids, you know. However, I soon changed my mind when they pointed what looked to be a gun at me. I was frozen to the spot."

"Did they say anything to you?" asked the reporter.

"They told me that I was trespassing on their territory. That they had taken the tree to Mars to examine it. If I behaved myself and promised not to say anything, they'd let me go. I can tell you, I promised them all right. They

were right ugly things, very scary."

"What did they look like?" said the reporter, attempting to get a better picture of things.

"They were green," the man went on, "and they had pointed noses and were about 7 feet tall. I was scared. It was very scary."

"Thank you," said the reporter, turning away from the man "as you have just heard, this man had a face to face meeting with these aliens and it was not a very nice meeting either. He considers that he is lucky to be alive. Over to you Mark."

John, Penny and Jimmy sat in astonishment as they watched the television report in John's bedroom.

"The liar," said Jimmy, becoming a little angry. "He's lying through his teeth. I can't believe he's made up such a pack of lies."

"He said we had a gun," said Penny, feeling quite shocked.

"Well, I'm just glad that he didn't see where we went," added John. "That could have been quite tricky."

Since the discovery of the tree, the place had been swamped with news reporters from all over the Country. There were television cameras everywhere and the children were reluctant to go over the fields just in case the man was there and recognised them.

"He couldn't have recognised us," said John, "or the police and news people would have been knocking on our doors."

"That's true," said Jimmy, "but fancy telling stories like that."

Jimmy had come round to the Carter's house because he was fed up hearing about the tree. They had a television in practically every room at home and it had been getting on his nerves. It had been no different when John's dad had let him in.

"Have you heard about the tree?" Mr Carter had asked him, "it looks like the Martians have really come doesn't it?"

"John," Penny asked, "can't you wish that the reporters and everyone else will go away?

"I could do," he answered, "but let's keep them guessing for a while. They'll never guess that we did it and if they did, I'd wish that they'd forget all about it."

"It'll drive me mad," said Jimmy, "but I agree, it's a good laugh. What are we going to do today?"

"I think we'll keep a low profile and just bum around here," John replied, "what do you say?"

They all agreed on this. In fact, they did the same on the Sunday, preferring to keep their heads down until they had to venture out to school the next day.

"Okay, we'll have no talk about Martians or oak trees vanishing and then reappearing," said the head teacher in the morning assembly, his balding head catching the reflection of the sun through a window. "There is absolutely no truth in such a claim and it will be proven before very long. Now have I made myself clear?"

"Yes sir," the whole school shouted in unison.

"I'm glad to hear it. At the end of the day, it will probably come to light that some silly child is responsible for such a prank. I hope, may I add, that it is not someone from this school because their feet will not touch the ground. Now off to your lessons."

"*H*e's a right big head," said Jimmy as they filed out of the hall into the main corridor of the school. "Who does he think he is?"

"He's the head and that's who he knows he is," replied John. "Don't worry though. I've got a little plan for our head teacher."

*A*t break time, John went into the toilet and locked himself in one of the small closets. Taking the book out of his pocket, he began to make a wish that the head teacher's car would change colour.

"I wish that the colour will change from green to purple," he said and opened the door to walk out of the toilet.

"Who were you talking to in there?" asked a boy that John had not seen before.

"I wasn't talking to anyone," John replied politely.

"Yes you were," the boy continued, "I heard you. Who were you talking to?"

"I've told you," John replied, trying to remain patient with this newcomer.

"I heard you say something about changing a colour from green to purple," the boy went on. "What's that all about?"

"Who are you anyway?" asked John, "I've never seen you before. Have you just started at the school?"

"My names Aaron Walker," he said, "we've just moved into the area. It's my first day here."

"I'm John, it's good to see you," said John moving to shake his hand.

Aaron grabbed John's hand and began to twist his arm until John felt like screaming.

"Tell me who you were talking to and what the colour changes were all about," said Aaron in an aggressive tone.

"Get off me you thug," shouted John, almost crying with the pain.

Just then the door opened and Jimmy walked in.

"Oh you're here," Jimmy said, "I've been looking...hey what do you think you're doing?"

Jimmy lunged at Aaron and together they managed to get the bully off John and shoved into the corner.

"You'll be sorry for that," Aaron spat at Jimmy. "You'll really regret that you messed about with Aaron Walker. And you, John, whatever your name is, we'll have this conversation again soon."

With that, Aaron stormed out of the toilet.

"What was all that about?" asked Jimmy concerned.

John filled him in on what had happened and they decided that they had better be careful in the future. This new boy, Aaron, appeared to be a nasty character.

*T*he break time was almost over as they both walked out into the playground. Something was happening at the far end of the play area, near the car park. A large crowd had gathered and there was a lot of laughing and joking going on.

The boys hurried over to get a better view. John's eyes nearly popped out of his head as he drew nearer. What he saw, was the very irate head teacher shouting about his car. It was then that John noticed that the head's car had been turned to purple.

"Who's been near my car," the head shouted. "My car was green. Now it's a horrible purple. I'll find out who is responsible for this and their feet won't touch the ground, I can assure you of that."

In the scuffle in the toilets, John had forgotten that he had wished for this to happen. It came as a complete shock to him, one that he wished, hadn't happened.

"Did you do this?" asked Jimmy smiling.

"I'll tell you later," said John.

"Yes," said another voice, "you'll tell me too."

John spun around to see the leering face of Aaron Walker standing very close to them both.

"I knew you were up to something and I know you did this," Aaron continued. "I'm going to love beating the daylights out of you until you tell me the truth. You see, I'm bigger than you and what you've got, I want."

"Get out of here," Jimmy said squaring up to Aaron. "Lay one hand on him and you'll take us both on."

"Good, then I'll see you both later, "Aaron said, walking off to his lessons smiling.

"That kid gives me the creeps," said Jimmy. "There's something very strange about him."

"I know," replied John," trying to control his heart beat.

Seven

*A*aron Walker was a little older than John and Jimmy having just turned 10. He was around four feet tall with quite broad shoulders and this gave him a slight edge over them; he was stronger and bigger. He was a strange looking boy with a very pale face that tended to give him an eerie appearance.

Not a lot was known about him. Apparently, his family were thought to have moved into the area over the past few weeks and he had been enrolled at The John Williams Primary School. Today had been his first day there and he certainly had made an impact with some children.

"I don't want to be at this school," he muttered to himself, as he sat down at his desk, "but I'm going to make my mark, and fast. Those boys will wish they had never seen me by the time that I'm finished with them."

*M*eanwhile, the head teacher was trying to come to terms with the new look that his car had. Several of the teaching staff thought that it was hilarious and joked behind his back.

"How on earth can this have been done," he pondered, walking back to his office.

"What are we going to do about Aaron?" asked Jimmy as he and John walked to their next lesson. "He's proving to be a pain. Can't you wish something on him?"

"He's a problem I agree," replied John, "but I don't want to use the little red book in a wrong way. It's okay having a joke with some people but I draw the line at violence."

"You could always get him in trouble with the head for something," said Penny, after they had given her the details of their confrontation with Aaron. "It sounds like he needs to be taught a lesson. What about letting him get the blame for the head's car?"

"I need to think it through," answered John. "I'll come up with something, don't worry."

The rest of the day at school went by without any further incidents. The head teacher was still ranting and raving about his car and threatening to have the whole school stay in for a couple of hours to teach them a lesson. However, he had no foundation to his claim that it was one of the pupils.

He had considered calling the police but he struggled with what he could say to them. The fact that his car had changed colour could not be denied. The problem was, it was a perfect spray job. No pupil would have been able to do that, especially in broad daylight. He also did not want to draw attention to the media. There was still the incident of the tree that had not been resolved. The general public had been forced to consider that Martians had been responsible for that. He definitely did not want the media crawling all over the school premises. He had a good reputation with the education department to preserve.

"I'll just have to accept this," he mumbled to himself.

John and Penny were late getting out of school. They had been doing art work and Penny had been completely lost in her work that she

45

couldn't possibly stop when the bell went.

"I've got to finish this last piece of the sky," Penny said, "and then I'll have to clear up. The brushes will go hard if I don't wash them off."

John decided to give her a hand and Jimmy joined him. It took about a further 20 minutes before they walked around the rear of the school to make their way home.

They were just near the bike sheds when Aaron Walker came in front of them.

"Well, well, well," he said, "if it isn't my little friends."

"We're not your friends," said Jimmy, always the first to rise to a challenge.

"Shut up stupid," shrieked Aaron. "I'm speaking and will have no one interrupt me."

"Who do you think you are?" Penny said, feeling very agitated by the tone of this boy who she had never seen before.

"Shut up and go and play with your dolls, little girl," Aaron said. My business is with these little boys, not you. Get off home."

"Don't talk to my sister like that," said John, suddenly feeling the courage to retaliate.

"What are you going to do about it John?" taunted Aaron. "Are you going to change me to purple like you did the head's car?"

"Don't be so silly," John replied. "I had nothing to do with that."

"I heard you in the toilets," continued Aaron. "You were on about changing something from green into purple. It's strange that just after that the head's car had changed colour. Now I figure that you were responsible so let me have what you've got and I'll leave you alone."

"I haven't *got* anything," said John, becoming frustrated now.

Aaron made a grab for John and threw him on the ground. As he did so, he ripped one of the pockets from his school jacket depositing the contents on the ground alongside John.

"What's this?" asked Aaron bending down to pick up the little red book. "Wow, it looks like I've found the secret to your success."

"Give it back," said Jimmy throwing himself at Aaron.

"I told you to shut up," said Aaron, pushing him back against the bike shed, which resulted in Jimmy stumbling backwards among some bikes.

"Hey, what do you think you're doing?" shouted a voice from the doorway that the children had not long walked through.

"Stay where you are, all of you."

Within seconds, a small chap possibly aged around 30, came running up to them.

"I'm Mr Leonard, the new Science teacher," he said. "Now, give me your names and tell me what's going on here."

"These kids attacked me and tried to mug me," shouted Aaron, "I was just defending myself."

"I don't think so," said Mr Leonard, "I am satisfied from what I saw that you were the one that did the attacking. Now what's it about?"

John, Penny and Jimmy all began speaking at once and in the end, Mr Leonard had to stop them.

"One at a time please," he said. "Now what happened?"

John tried to explain that they had been messing around. He didn't want to 'dob Aaron in'. He just wanted to get home and have no more trouble.

"No, that's not what I saw," said Mr Leonard. "What's that in your hand Aaron?"

"Oh nothing," Aaron replied, trying to put the book into his pocket.

"It's ours," shouted Penny, "he stole it from us. That's what the fighting was about."

"No I didn't," said Aaron, "anyway, John turned the head teacher's car from green to purple and I think he used this book to do it with."

"Really," said Mr Leonard. "How did he do that? Did he paint the car with the book?"

"Not with the book, no," Aaron said, feeling embarrassed. "He used, like, you know, a a spell or something."

"How stupid can you get?" shouted Jimmy. "That's the most stupid thing I've ever heard."

"Okay, okay," said Mr Leonard, "I've heard enough for now. Give John the book, Aaron, NOW! Then get off home. I'll see you straight after the assembly in the morning. If you touch John, Penny or Jimmy, you'll be in serious trouble. Do I make myself clear?"

"Yes," said Aaron.

"Yes what Aaron?" Mr Leonard said.

"Yes sir," Aaron replied, walking off up the path to the main gate.

"Right you three," said Mr Leonard, "give him a few minutes and get off home yourself. Do you live far?

"Just down the road, about 150 yards," said Penny.

"Tell you what," he said, "I'll walk with you just in case our friend tries it on again."

John, Penny and Jimmy, had made it home with no further problems. They had gone home to get changed and to wait for their tea and was now sitting in Jimmy's bedroom going over the events of the day.

"He's a really nice bloke," said Penny, breaking the silence.

"Who is?" Jimmy and John both said in unison.

"Mr Leonard," she replied. "If it hadn't been for him, you'd have both been beaten up and Aaron would have taken the book. I think he's nice."

"You fancy him," you mean," said her brother.

"Don't talk so silly," said Penny, "I think he's just nice, that's all."

"He's all right," agreed Jimmy," and let's face it, we'd have been in real trouble if he hadn't have turned up when he did."

"Yea, that's true," said John. "That Aaron's a nasty piece of work."

"I saw him having a go at someone else earlier today," said Penny. "He practically picked a boy up and threw him on the grass. He's has strong as an ox. He really gives me the creeps."

"Yes, me too," said Jimmy.

What are we going to do?" asked Penny. "He knows about the book now and it'll only be a matter of time before he takes it off you John."

"No he won't," said John. "From now on, I'm going to leave it where I found it, under the floorboards. We'll only get it out when we want to use it again."

"Have you got it with you now?" asked Jimmy.

"Yes, I have," replied John. "Just for tonight though."

"Don't you think you ought to wish that the head's car is returned to its original colour?" asked Jimmy. "He's going on and on about it. It'll only be a matter of time before he finds out about the book, especially if Aaron tells him."

"Yes, I suppose," said John. "It would have been nice to change the colour again though, wouldn't it? You know orange with green spots on or something."

"That would be great," said Jimmy. "Do you think we could get away with it?"

"We could, if we did everything from here," replied John. "There's no way the head could come into our house and look around for the book. Anyway, it's Aaron's word against ours and he hasn't made a very good start, has he?"

*T*he children thought it through for a little while. They all felt that it would be great to keep the joke going with the head teacher for a little longer. They also thought about teaching Aaron a lesson and finally came up with an idea.

"Let's wish that Aaron's hair turns white," said John, "that'll give us all a laugh and teach him a lesson. Also let's do as I said, and turn the heads car into an orange one with green spots on it. He won't know it's us and if Aaron threatens to tell him that it was us, we'll tell him that something worse will happen to him."

"It's a bit dodgy," said Penny, "but as long as you leave the book in your bedroom, it'll be safe and no one will be able to prove we've done anything wrong."

"What about Aaron?" said Jimmy. "He'll go mad when he sees his hair and he'll know that we've done it."

"Again, he'll have no proof," said John, "and we'll just stay together."

With that, John performed the wishes. There was no way at this stage to check that the wishes had been granted. They agreed to meet up at 8am in the morning, to walk the short distance to the school and then see what happened.

John and Penny went home and John went straight to his bedroom and placed the book under the floorboard where he had found it.

Eight

"*W*as everything okay last night?" asked Mr Leonard as he walked through the school gates, spotting the children.

"Yes," we had no problem, thanks sir," replied John.

"What's with this book?" Mr Leonard asked, "Aaron was saying that you used it to turn the head's car a different colour. What was all that about?"

"Oh, he's just an idiot," said Jimmy, trying to divert the teacher's interest away from where the conversation was going. "By the way sir, do you know anything about Mars?"

"What Planet Mars?" he replied. "Yes, I know the basics. Why do you want to know about that?"

"It was just a conversation we had last night," said Penny, keeping the pretence going. "We were wondering if there was life up there, especially as everyone seems to be thinking that Martians were responsible for the old oak tree situation that was on the tele last week."

"Oh that," Mr Leonard replied. "Yes, that was rather strange wasn't it? Mind you, no stranger than what happened to the head's car yesterday."

"Yes," said John, "that was bizarre. Do you think that was Martians too?"

"I don't know what to think," he said, "but if you want to know about Mars, why don't you meet me in the lab this afternoon. I've got a free period from 2pm."

"So have we," said Penny, "our teacher, Mr Jackson is still off sick."

"Then I'll see you later then," said Mr Leonard working towards the main entrance of the school. "I'll clear it with the head."

Over the other side of the playground, near the car park, there was a small crowd of children crowding round a car.

"Oh no," here we go," said Penny, feeling a mixture of excitement and embarrassment. I think your wish has come true again."

They walked over to have a closer look. The head was nowhere in sight when they reached the crowd. His car was however, and it was a wonderful, bright colour of orange with large green spots all over it that gave the impression that the car had measles.

"Oh flipping heck," cried John turning away from the spectacle, "let's go over to the other side."

"Awesome," said Jimmy, staring at the car. "My dad would love his car to be like this."

"Well, leave me out of it," said John, walking away.

Just then, they spotted Aaron. He was standing over near the doorway of the school wearing a large woolly hat that was pulled down nearly over the whole of his head.

"Aaron," said Jimmy, "why are you wearing that flipping hat this weather? You must be roasting in it."

"You know why," he said, pulling the three of them closer into the doorway. "Now turn my hair back to its original colour, or you're dead."

"We don't know what you're on about," said John, trying not to smirk at the comical face of Aaron, especially when he saw a glimpse of white hair poking out at the back of his neck. "Do you think we've done this as well?"

"You know you have," answered Aaron, feeling desperate now because the bell was about to go and he would have to take his hat off. "Turn my hair back to dark blond and we'll forget the whole thing. Come on get your magic book out."

I haven't got the book with me," said John, "and anyway, it's not magic at all. It's in your imagination."

Just then the bell went and they all filed up into their lines ready to walk into school. Jimmy glanced round to see where Aaron was. He just caught sight of the back of him as he walked quickly out of the school.

"Good riddance," he thought, although he did feel a little guilty about it all.

*T*he head teacher sat in his office. He was perplexed. In fact, he was angry. How on earth had the colour of his car been changed again? It was crazy. It had been in the garage since he got home last night. He had risen early this morning and planned to get into school before anyone else in order to avoid any further comments. As he had opened his up and over garage door, he had been totally shocked to find that it had changed to orange with horrible big green spots on it.

"I can't believe this is happening," he had almost cried. "What have I done to deserve this? The car's been locked in the garage all night. No one could have got to it. The door was still locked and yet this."

He had gone back into his house with the intention of taking his wife's car to avoid the ribbing that he would get later at school.

"You know I need the car," his wife had said, "I've got to go into town for an appointment."

"Can't you take mine?" he had pleaded over and over again.

"Darling, you've got to be joking. I wouldn't be seen dead in that," she had replied.

Knowing that he was getting nowhere with his pleadings and realising that if he didn't move quickly, he would not be there early, he had climbed into the psychedelic thing on wheels, and had roared off into the early morning.

"It's the 4th planet from the sun in the Solar system," said Mr Leonard to the children, who had gathered in his lab as arranged earlier, "and it's named after Mars, the Roman God of war."

"Is there life up there?" asked Jimmy.

"Scientists think there could be," Mr Leonard continued, knocking over a Bunsen burner as he waved his arms around. "Mind you, there is no liquid water up there due to the low atmospheric pressure, so it would be a little grim and the whole planet is subject to violent dust storms."

"If there is life on Mars, how would the Martians exist without water?" asked Penny.

"Oh there's plenty of water around," Mr Leonard said, "but it is solid ice. This is plentiful because there are two polar ice caps made largely of ice. There is though a large supply of water under the surface, but it's at a great depth."

"How do they drink then?" asked John, quite concerned.

"Well you can melt ice and also suck it, so I suppose it may be done that way," Mr Leonard continued "there are also no oceans or seas like we have on earth has. There are river valleys but they are dry. The water is way down under the ground."

"It sounds like a bleak place to live," said Jimmy.

"I think it's a fabulous place," said Mr Leonard enthusiastically,

"There are mountains, and one of them is the Olympus Mons which is massive. It's the highest known mountain in the whole Solar system, and actually it is a volcano. And then there is the Valles Marineris."

"What's that?" asked John, really becoming interested now.

"It's a very large canyon," Mr Leonard said. "You think the Grand Canyon is big, but it has nothing on this chappie. Its length is 4000 km and reaches a depth of 7km. When you compare the Grand Canyon, which is 446 km in length and 2km deep, you can see that it is massive."

"Would we be able to breathe if we went up there?" asked Penny.

"That is debateable," said Mr Leonard, screwing his eyes up as if he was thinking hard. "I would say, because of the low atmospherics and the presence of methane gas, one would need breathing equipment. But who knows? One thing is for sure, it is an exciting place to be. What with the large craters, volcanoes, valleys and deserts, there would be lots to explore.

"Is it too hot for humans to land on there?" said John, trying to gain as much information as possible.

"On the contrary," he replied, "the day up there is slightly longer than what we are used to but it has light and darkness, you know, day and night, and there are very cold spots and very warm. It would be a matter of finding the right spot."

"Wow," said Penny, "how is it that you know so much about the place?"

"I've studied Mars for many years," he replied, "ever since I was a boy and dreamed of one day going up in a spaceship, probably like you have been doing."

"We'd love to go," said John, "it's my dream."

"Mine too," said Jimmy, getting a taste for the place.

"Hmm," was all that Penny said. She did not want to commit herself, knowing what John had in mind.

"Well that's it, I'm afraid," said Mr Leonard, "It's your home time and I've some marking to do. I hope it's been interesting."

"It's been fabulous," said John, "thank you so much sir. If we go, we'll be sure to ask you to come with us."

"I'd be forced to accept," Mr Leonard said laughing.

Nine

*I*t had been a dreary day and the head teacher was glad that he was eventually driving home to the peace and quiet of his home. He was still bitter about the colouring of his car. However, for the life of him, he hadn't a clue how it could have happened.

As he turned right at the intersection towards where he lived, he saw Mr Jackson walking along the pavement. As he pulled up to have a chat with him he couldn't help notice the anxiety that was spread all over his face.

"Are you okay Terry?" he asked after winding his window down.

"Oh hi," Mr Jackson replied. "I haven't been too good. I'm off to see the doctor."

"Hop in," the head replied, "I'm going past the surgery, I'll give you a lift."

They drove on in silence for a little while, both of them lost in their thoughts until they came to the surgery which was slightly set back from the road.

"Here we are then Terry," said the head. "What time's your appointment?"

"I'm early actually," Terry replied, "but I'll go in and read a magazine until they call me in. By the way, what's happened to the car? I didn't know you went in for the psychedelic look."

"It's a long story," said the head, and went into great detail about the last few days.

"I just can't figure it out," the head teacher said.

"Well, I'll be," said Terry, "I wonder?" He then began to tell the head teacher about the words vanishing from the chalkboard and then returning. At the end of this account, they both sat staring at each other."

"This is why I was seeing my GP," said Terry, "I thought I was cracking up."

"Well I don't think you need bother now," said the head. "It looks like we have both been the victims of some strange behaviour. Let's look at it. First there was the oak tree. That vanished from the field and then returned again. Then your writing vanished and that returned. My car has turned from the nice green that I chose, to purple and now to this ridiculous psychedelic look. They say the oak tree was the work of Martians. I doubted this at first but now, I don't know.

"It really is bizarre," replied Terry. "I really thought I was going mad. I can't tell you how relieved I am. Wait till the media gets hold of this little lot. They'll have a heyday."

"Now, that's what I don't want Terry," said the head teacher. "The school's up for an award this year, I don't want anything to jeopardise that."

"Well we can't let this get out of hand," said Terry, "Things could go bizarre if we don't do something about it."

"I agree," said the head. "But can I suggest that we sit on this and if things continue to happen, I'll have a word with education and see what they advise."

"Well as long as you do," said Terry. "I can't tell you what I've been through these past few days."

"I think I know, to a degree," the head replied. "Do you want me to drop you at home as you won't need your appointment now?"

"No, that's okay," Terry said, feeling very relieved, "I'm going to have a leisurely stroll back home and have a peaceful night for the first time this week."

Aaron Walker stood outside of the Carter's house waiting to see if he could see any of the children. He was very bitter towards them after the day that he'd had. He had not gone into the school because he would not have been able to face all of the rude comments because of his white hair. Instead, he had managed to get hold of a small bottle of hair dye and had spent the biggest part of the day, trying to put his hair back to its original colour.

The result wasn't too bad. His natural colouring was dark blond. The hair dye had turned him a darker colour, almost brown. However, it was better than the dazzling white that he had woken up to.

His main aim though, was to get hold of the book. He had nearly had it the other day. If it hadn't of been for the science teacher, he would have been home and dry. He walked down the road pleased that he had found their home. It was now just a matter of time. It would take some careful planning but he was confident he could do it.

"If I can only get hold of it," he thought, "it would change my life."

"Have we heard from Taneka yet?" Zelmut asked his trusty servant Yermin.

"We have your Highness," replied Yermin. "He is in place and has located the book. He has a plan and the plan will be successful, you can be sure of that. It will soon be in your hands your Highness."

"Good," said Zelmut, smiling broadly as he strutted across the tiled floor of his headquarters thinking of the power that would soon be his, and his only.

The children were thrilled with the thoughts of going to Mars. Even Penny, who had been very apprehensive at first, was now catching the excitement.

"We need to plan the trip very carefully," said John as they walked the short distance to the playground. "We want it to be perfect, so we don't want any problems."

"When shall we go?" asked Jimmy, wanting to get there as soon as he could. "Can't we go today? We'd miss the lesson with old Jackson then."

"I wish," said Penny," he's going to be groaning on about this Thomas Hardy fellow again."

"I'd forgotten about that," said John, "he's back now isn't he? Still, we can't rush this, I want to speak with Mr Leonard and get some more info first."

"It would be great to take him with us, wouldn't it?" said Penny. "I mean, he's an authority on the place."

"Yea," said John, "he'd be the type of person needed on a trip like we're planning. He'd never agree though and it would mean telling him about the book."

As the bell went, they walked into their lesson to face the irritable Mr Jackson.

"*I*'ve wanted to speak with you," said Mr Leonard, running to keep up with them as they made their way home. "I can't think of anything except Mars. You guys have really fired me up about it. Do you fancy meeting up in the lab again tomorrow night after school."

"Yes, that would be great," said John excitedly, "there's lots more we need to know."

"You sound very serious," said Mr Leonard, "If I didn't know differently, I'd say that you have a trip planned."

"You never know," said Jimmy as the children walked out of the gate in the direction of home.

The children decided that they would meet up at the old oak tree after tea. John was feeling that there was a lot of planning to do and wanted to be out of the way of his parent's, just in case they overheard these important plans.

*B*y now, all of the television crews had returned back to their studios. The tree would have to remain unexplained as there was other media demanding their attention. It was good to have the fields to play on without the crowds and the children walked over to the little hill that they often sat on to talk about this and that.

"I think we should go very soon," said John seriously. "We've got the meeting with Mr Leonard tomorrow night. We'll get all the info we need and plan to go on Saturday. What do you think?"

"Saturday," said Jimmy, "Man Utd are playing Chelsea on Saturday and it's on the tele. We'll miss it. Can't we go on Monday? I hate Monday's"

"Yea, I do too," said Penny, "but not as much as football."

"I'd forgotten about that," said John, a strong supporter of Manchester United. "We'll make it Monday then."

"What are you scheming about now?" said Aaron Walker, walking up from behind startling them."

"What do you want?" asked Jimmy, not hiding his feelings about how he felt about the high and mighty Aaron Walker.

"You know what I want," whispered Aaron in his ear. "I want that book and I want it now."

"Nice hair style Aaron," Penny said sniggering. "That dark brown really suits you."

"Watch it you stupid little girl," sneered Aaron. "I've got to teach you all a lesson for what you did to me."

"We didn't do anything," said John, "it's all in your imagination."

"Give me the book and I'll let you off turning my hair white," Aaron went on.

"How many times do you have to be told," said Penny, "we didn't do anything to you."

"Give me the book!" shouted Aaron.

"It's at home," said John getting frustrated now. "I tell you what though, if you don't leave us alone, we'll do more than turn your hair white that's for sure."

With that, Aaron dived on John and began wrestling him over and over on the grass. Without any hesitation, Jimmy jumped on top of Aaron frantically trying to get the bully off his friend. However, neither of them were a match for the incredible strength that Aaron had. He just threw Jimmy off his back and continued to try to hurt John.

Just then, a man walking his dog noticed the scuffle. He came running over to stop them, his dog barking furiously at Aaron, who by now had a most horrible look on his face.

"Leave the kids alone you bully," he shouted at Aaron, trying to keep his dog from doing Aaron some mischief. "I don't know where you live but get out of here now or I'll set my dog on you."

Aaron, just a little shocked at the intrusion, stared at the man and then the dog, who by now was barking out of control. He reluctantly decided to go on his way. He wanted to rip the man and the dog apart with his bare hands, but noticing other people in the field, who were by now coming over to find out what was happening, he ran off.

"Are you okay?" the man asked John as he pulled him to his feet.

"Yea, I'm fine," said John shaking from the shock of it all. "Thanks for helping. It was just a disagreement, that's all. It's nothing to worry about."

"Well I think you ought to report the blighter to the police," the man went on. "He could have done you some real damage if I hadn't run over. Do you live around here? I'll take you home and explain to your parents."

"No, we live a good way from here," said John lying to protect their whereabouts. "We'll be okay though, don't worry."

With that, John, who was by now covered in straw and feeling quite sore from where Aaron had thumped him in the stomach, walked away with the others to the general direction of their homes.

"We've got to do something about that idiot," said Jimmy, embarrassed that he didn't have the strength to help his best friend.

"We could take him to Mars with us and leave him there," said Penny.

"Hmm, that's an idea," said John trying to focus on the path he was walking upon.

Ten

"*I*'ve thought of nothing else," said Mr Leonard, leaning on the heavy counter in the science laboratory. "I'm completely enthralled by the whole idea of Planet Mars."

The children, especially John, had recovered from their scuffle with Aaron the previous night and were eager to pursue their plans of going to Mars. They had been in heavy discussion during the day about the subject and managing to dodge the intimidating figure of Aaron, had decided, because they trusted him, that they would tell Mr Leonard about the book and all that had happened since.

"Yes the whole prospect of Mars and even a visit, is something I've dreamed about since I was a child."

"We need to talk to you sir," said John, "and it may sound a little far-fetched, but it's the truth.

The children then went on to tell him about John finding the book, John turning into a fly, the cakes and everything else that had happened since he had found the book.

"You mean it is you who are responsible for the old oak tree vanishing like it did and the head's car changing colour?" asked Mr Leonard completely astounded. "That is absolutely amazing."

"You won't say anything will you?" said John, wondering if they'd done the right thing. "We'd be in big trouble with everyone if you did and we'd never get to Mars."

"No don't worry," said Mr Leonard reassuringly. "You have my word and anyway, the book is our ticket to Mars."

You'd really like to come with us then?" asked Penny.

"You try and stop me," replied Mr Leonard. "As I've said before, it's my dream to go there and now we have the opportunity, I really can't wait."

"When shall we go then?" asked Jimmy, becoming excited at the whole thing happening very soon.

"I think we should plan to go as soon as we can," said Mr Leonard, "but it is John's decision. He's in control as far as I'm concerned."

John began to feel very proud that he had been recognised as the leader of this expedition, in fact the commander. He felt that he should slip into this role and make very precise plans.

"Right," he said, "it's Wednesday today, how about Friday night after school. I'll bring the book in with me and we'll meet in this lab when the bell goes and off we go."

"Man Utd are playing the next day," said Jimmy horrified."

"I know Jimmy," said John with an air of importance, "but some things have to take a back seat. No it's Friday and that is final."

"Good," said Mr Leonard, "let's meet here after the bell goes and take it from there."

"What if we don't like it there?" asked Penny suddenly panicking, "Or if we can't breathe or there are monsters or whatever?"

"Then we'll wish ourselves back," said John, reassuringly. "We are very much in control of the whole thing, as long as we keep the book."

With the whole situation finalised and arranged, the children set off home in a state of excitement and apprehension.

It took ages for Friday to come round. As it often happens when exciting things are about to become reality, time seems to stand still and it appears that the event will never happen.

However, Friday had come and the children were sitting in their classroom waiting for the bell to ring that would signal it was home time. When the bell finally rang, they were startled and their hearts began to race at the thought of their journey into the unknown.

They quickly made their way to the science lab and were relieved to find Mr Leonard waiting for them, equally as excited as they were themselves.

"Well, this is it then," he said. "No turning back now, hey?"

"No," said John, his heart still pounding with the excitement.

"Have you got the book?" asked Mr Leonard.

"Oh, flipping heck," said John. "I've left it in my bag in the cloakroom. I'll go and get it."

The cloakroom was only just around the corner from the science lab and John raced round there to get it. He picked it off the rail, checked that the book was still inside and went on his way back to the lab.

"What are you up to punk?" asked Aaron, who had been walking along the opposite corridor. "Have you got my book yet?"

John tried to ignore him and shoved past the heavy physique towards the door of the lab. Just then, Aaron made a grab for John's bag. Fortunately, John had wrapped his arm around the strap and had a firm hold of it.

"Let it go Aaron," shouted John, desperately trying to hang on to the bag.

"It's mine," said Aaron, "the books inside, I know it is. Let me have it and I'll not hurt you."

Just then, Mr Leonard and the others, hearing voices outside in the corridor, came out and saw what was happening. Mr Leonard, with great strength, pulled the bag from Aaron and frog-marched him into the lab.

"We're going to have to do something about your aggression, young man," Mr Leonard whispered to Aaron.

"What are we going to do with him?" said Jimmy, "he's been a pain in the backside since the day we met him."

"Let's tie him up," said John, "and then get on with our plans."

"No," said Mr Leonard, "we don't want to treat violence with violence and it would be unfair to leave a young boy here over the weekend."

"Let's take him with us and leave him there, like I said earlier," said Penny. "He's not going to keep silent about this and at least we can keep an eye on him if he's with us."

"Where are you going?" asked Aaron.

"We're going to Mars," said Jimmy and you're coming with us, whether you like it or not."

"I knew you were up to something," sneered Aaron. "Take me with you then, it won't bother me, but I won't be left there, it'll be you punks that are."

"Now stop that," said Mr Leonard. "Aaron, we've decided that you're coming with us. It can be a pleasant trip, with you behaving yourself. Or, it can be unpleasant with you tied up and masking tape over your mouth to keep you quiet. You choose."

Aaron reluctantly elected to behave himself, for now anyway. He had plans and he would succeed. He had made up his mind about that.

*T*he four of them gathered around John as he took the little red book into his hands.

His hands shook as he began to speak and wish that they were all transported to the illustrious and fascinating world of Planet Mars.

"I wish that we are all taken to Planet Mars right now," said John with a trembling voice that could be plainly heard by the others, although John had tried very hard to disguise this.

Just then, the place went all dark and for the first time since John had the book, he was not the only one to see this. The colours that they all witnessed were amazing, flashes of red, purple orange and green appeared to flicker around the small science lab like they were in a discotheque. There was a loud hissing noise that threatened to blow their ear drums apart and they all felt themselves flying at an incredible pace that took their breath away. And has quickly as it had started, peace began to settle down and they were deposited on the ground with a slight bump."

"Wow, that was amazing," shouted Jimmy, unable to contain himself.

"Be quiet," said Mr Leonard urgently. "We've got to check this place out and discover what we're up against."

"Yes," said John, trying to affirm control of what he felt was his mission. "Where do you think we are sir?"

"Well," said Mr Leonard, "this is definitely Mars and that is Olympus Mons in the distance."

The children followed the direction he was pointing and noticed the large, awesome mountain that he referred to, coming up out of the ground like some creepy monster. It was so large, they could not see the top of the mountain and they estimated that it was at least 20 miles away.

They had obviously landed on Mars at night time. The place was dark but lit up with many stars. For a moment, they could have believed that they were on earth, just looking up into the heavens.

The ground was very different from home. There was a thick coating of dark red dust, possibly to a depth of about 8 inches, all over as far as they could see. The dust was like talcum powder and it made walking very difficult, especially as the dust covered a hard rock, crater like surface that had sharp pieces sticking up every now and then.

The first thing they noticed was that they could breathe. Everything they had learned about space pointed to the fact that people would need to wear special suits in order to be able to breathe in the atmosphere. However, here they were, dressed in the clothes they had been wearing on Planet Earth and they were okay.

They had all remembered to bring a coat, just in case the place was cold. That is, except Aaron, who had had no idea that he would be making such a journey. However, Mr Leonard had thought of that and had taken a coat that had been left in the cloak room, so that Aaron would be warm.

The place was absolutely breathtaking, with mountains, or volcanoes as Mr Leonard had told them, all around. There were also massive craters scattered all around and very deep valleys and like river formations with no water in them.

Even though there were thick blocks of ice everywhere they looked, the temperature, they found, was quite acceptable and this all added to the mystery of Planet Mars.

"I think it would be wise to make our way to Olympus Mons," said Mr Leonard, "it will give us a vantage point and protect us should a dust storm start up."

"It's a long walk," said Penny, "especially in this dust. It'll take us ages."

"Better we start now then," said Mr Leonard, is tone a little sharper than it had originally been.

*T*hey had been walking for what seemed hours and were still no nearer to the mountain when Penny sat down for a rest.

"Can we take a break sir?" she asked Mr Leonard.

"No we must keep going," replied Mr Leonard. "I know this area and it's not very nice to be out in a dust storm I can assure you."

"How do you know sir?" asked Aaron, who had been quiet since they arrived.

"It's just what I've learned from the internet," Mr Leonard replied. "Apparently, the dust can cover everything over. We could be buried in this stuff if we were caught in it."

"What are those things over there," asked Penny, pointing in the direction of some small mountains. "Not the mountains, but the big holes underneath. Are they caves?"

"Yes they are," replied the teacher, "the entrances are massive, between 100 to 252 metres wide and they go to a great depth once inside."

"Can we have a look?" asked John, "after all this is supposed to be enjoyable, not just a route march."

"I suppose it won't hurt said Mr Leonard.

They were just about fifty yards from the entrance to one of the caves when they heard the most terrifying scream as something whizzed over their heads

"Get down quickly;" said Mr Leonard, "it's the Termans."

"The who..?" asked John feeling quite frightened.

"The Termans," Mr Leonard repeated, "they're the most feared of flying warriors, well creatures actually. They're not very nice I can tell you that. Let's try and make the entrance to that cave. We may be safe there."

There must have been about a dozen of these Termans buzzing around their heads and the battle was on to get to the cave as quickly as they could. They just made it as one of the Termans fired something like a rocket at them.

"Flipping heck, what was that," shouted Jimmy jumping to his feet and running further back into the cave.

"I think that was a blast of Antisum," said Mr Leonard. "The Martians use it as a weapon. If it hits the body, the body freezes like stone for about 30 minutes. By that time, you're captured and taken to their headquarters."

"What are these things?" shouted Jimmy from deeper in the cave. They look like motor bikes without wheels."

They all walked further into the cave to where Jimmy had shouted to them and looked down at the two strange objects he was pointing to.

"They're Troganbugs," said Mr Leonard. "They are the Martian's main means of travel up here on Planet Mars. They actually float about a foot off the ground and go at a great speed either forwards or backwards. They're a handy piece of kit I can assure you and they just work off the atmosphere, no petrol or other means of fuel needed."

They all sat on these strange objects, which were very much like a motor bike as Jimmy had suggested but had no wheels. They also had a sidecar attached that looked like it would carry two people.

"As you can see," said Mr Leonard, "they're capable of carrying 4 people; two on the vehicle itself and another two in the sidecar.

Mr Leonard showed them how to start them up. Within a few moments, the children were slowly buzzing around the interior of the cave having a great time.

"I think we need to stop for a while and rest." said Mr Leonard. "Once we've had a break, we can go and try and find something to eat. There should be plenty of choice up here but it's mainly berries I'm afraid. They're called Rogangoes. They look like a small orange but are plum coloured and extremely nice to eat. They grow on the sides of most rocks."

"How do you know all of this?" asked Penny suspiciously, "you wouldn't have got all of that information from the internet."

"I did a study on NASA and their findings on Mars," he replied. "It was very interesting. Come on, let's have a rest and then we'll set off again. I think the Termans have gone. They never venture into caves."

Eleven

"*H*e seems to know a lot, whispered Penny as Mr Leonard slept soundly.

"Yes, but he learnt it all from NASA, like he told us," said John in Mr Leonard's defence, "and don't forget that he's a teacher."

"Hmm, I'm not too sure," she said, "but we'll have to wait and see."

"Did you get a look at the Termans?" asked Jimmy, "they were awesome."

"They were flying too fast to see what they looked like," said Aaron, getting in on the conversation. "I didn't like the sound of them though."

"Cor, Aaron is frightened," said Jimmy.

"No I'm not," he said defensively, "it's just that it would be nice to know what we're up against. I mean, they were firing that Anti whatever at us."

"Antisum," said John, showing his intelligence. "It sounds pretty awful stuff if you're hit and I must agree with Aaron, it would be nice to know some more about these creepy things."

Just then, Mr Leonard stirred and sat up, scratching his head and stretching himself.

"Come on you guys," he said, "we must press forward but we'll stop and eat on the way."

They all mounted the Troganbugs, Mr Leonard taking one with Jimmy and Aaron as company and John and Penny in the other. Slowly they went forward to the mouth of the cave. It all looked quiet and after a few moments they set forth towards the great Olympus Mons.

The Troganbugs were great little things to drive and ride on. Floating about a foot off the ground and doing about 40 miles an hour, they hovered over the vast floor of Planet Mars.

After a short time, Mr Leonard pulled up at some rocks. He got off the Troganbug he was driving and walked towards a small clump of rocks.

"Ah, here we are," he said, pulling some strange looking things from off the side of the rocks. "Rogangoes, come on you chaps come and try some and get a chunk of ice to wash them down. They are really lovely."

The other four approached the rocks and followed the example of their teacher. At first, they were reluctant to try them. It was Aaron who went first and he was most impressed.

"They're lovely," he said, munching into these strange delights and biting a chunk of ice at the same time. "Try them."

John went next and the taste he felt in his mouth was adorable. "They're fantastic," he said to Jimmy and Penny as they too, pulled some of the Rogangoes from the rock.

After they had had their fill, they headed towards the awesome Olympus Mons. When they were about 10 miles from their destination, Mr Leonard pulled the Troganbug up close to some rocks. Just behind the rocks was the deepest canyon the children had ever seen. The sight of it took their breath away and they wondered how they would ever cross such a wide open space.

"This is the Valles Marineris that I told you about," said Mr Leonard. "It's a colossal size don't you think."

"How will we get over it?" asked Penny. "It's far too big."

"There's a rock bridge a little over a mile further down," said Mr Leonard said. "But you won't be going over it, only I will."

"What do you mean?" asked John. "Have we got to wait here for you or something?"

"You silly human people," said Mr Leonard in a very strange voice that made the children's hair stick up on their necks. "I am Taneka, the great warrior and I have been selected to bring the little red book back to Planet Mars. Up to now, my people have not been able to accurately pinpoint you because you haven't used the book since we arrived here. The Leoxostone can only pinpoint someone to within a few miles. Now though, they will not have to find you. You will be exterminated. In fact, you'll be thrown over this vast Martian spectacle, to your deaths. I am invincible."

The children were speechless as they looked at the person they had once trusted, the person who had practically begged them for a trip to Mars. As they looked at him, he took on another identity. His head began to shrink and he shrunk to about 4 feet in size. However, he had enormous broad shoulders that tugged at the maroon suit he somehow was now wearing. What frightened them the most was his face and his voice. The face had turned into a scaly, grey coloured horror, something like a mask that could be obtained in theatrical shops for people to dress up in. His voice sounded like it was coming from inside him, rather like a distorted radio. He was a very menacing sight.

"Give me the book, NOW!" Taneka, as the children now knew him, shouted.

"You've got to be joking," shouted Jimmy and John together," we'll never give you that no matter what you do, you traitor."

Taneka walked towards them with a can of Antisum in his hand. He was just going to squirt the boys, when there was a loud piercing scream that startled them all. Suddenly Aaron lunged at Taneka pushing him off the rock and deep into the canyon. His voice could be heard like a screaming laugh as he fell to his certain death.

"Flipping heck," said John, "that was brilliant Aaron. Well done. He's fallen into the canyon. He won't survive that, that's for sure. And if he did, it's so deep, he'll never get out. Come on let's get out of here and quickly."

The children, who were trembling with fear, climbed on one of the Troganbugs and went a short distance away from the canyon and stopped.

"Shouldn't we take both of the Troganbugs? Aaron asked suddenly. "We may need them."

That's a good idea," said John, "go and get it and we'll wait here for you."

Aaron had just made it to the other Troganbug, when the there was a mighty roar and Taneka was standing on the ledge in a threatening manner.

"I am invincible," he shouted. "You silly humans thought I was dead. But we Martians are immortal. We never die. I am the greatest of all warriors."

With that he struck Aaron on the side of the head knocking him almost to the edge of the canyon and jumped on the other Troganbug.

"I am going to claim my reward now," he screamed. "I will have nothing more to do with you. Pretty soon the warriors and the Termans will be looking for you. They will find you. But now, give me the book."

"Not a chance you traitor," shouted John.

"Then he will die and you will be responsible," Taneka shouted getting off the Troganbug and crouching down to the semi conscious Aaron, dragging him further to the edge of the canyon. "You will be murderers, responsible for the death of this pathetic creature."

Taneka picked Aaron up as if he was a ragged doll and held him above his head. He was ready to throw Aaron into the canyon.

"Wait," John shouted. "Put him down and I'll give you the book."

Taneka complied with John's request, placing Aaron roughly back onto the ground.

"Now walk away from Aaron," said John and I'll throw the book to you."

"This is as far as I will go," said Taneka, standing near the Troganbug.

John threw the book into the vehicle and raced over to Aaron quickly dragging him back to where the others were.

"Well done humans," said Taneka. I will be on my way now, to glory. I pity you though when the warriors and Termans come to attack you."

With that, he roared off into the early morning sunrise creating a massive cloud of dust.

Twelve

"Quickly, let's follow him," shouted John to the others. "He's getting away."

"We don't want to go after him, the Martians will get us," said Penny, "you heard what he said. We should be going back and hiding in the caves."

"We can't do that," said John, "the Termans and the warriors will never suspect that we are following Taneka. They will think that we've gone the other way, like you're suggesting. And anyway, he's got the book. We'll never get back home without it. Come one."

The four of them squeezed onto the Troganbug and raced up the canyon to try and find the bridge that Taneka had mentioned.

Meanwhile Zelmut rubbed his hands with glee. He had just heard that his warrior, Taneka had almost fulfilled his mission and was on his way to Olympus Mons.

"My faithful warrior is about to be rewarded beyond his wildest dreams." He said.

"He surely is the best," said Yermin, pleased that it was nearly all over. "Taneka has asked that we send out the warriors and the

Termans to exterminate the humans. Shall I do this, your Highness?"

"Yes," Zelmut replied, "but try and keep one of them alive. It would be good to find out how they live and what they're made of. We can then vaporise the human later."

"Your wish is my command, your Highness." said Yermin, bowing to Zelmut and leaving the room.

Taneka found the rock bridge and began to drive over it. He estimated it to be about 3 miles across the canyon. The greatest measurement was its length which he knew was 4000 km.

"Strange that it is so long and deep and yet only 3 miles wide," he thought, as he made the journey over the rough bridge which had no sides to it. He was so deep in thought that he failed to notice a high piece of rock jutting out in front of him. Too late, the Troganbug hit the rock with so much force that it threw Taneka forward and out of the vehicle. Taneka just had time to see the Troganbug, disappear over the side to the depths below.

"Drat it," he said. "Never mind, I will make my way on foot and will enter into the courts of the Olympus Mons in total glory."

Taneka failed to realise that he could have taken the little red book and wished to be there instantly.

"We must be gaining on him surely," shouted Jimmy, who was sitting behind John as they raced at about 50mph across the little bridge that they had found quite easily.

"He had about 5 minutes on us," John shouted back, "it's quite a head start on us, but we'll get him, that's for sure."

"What are we going to do if we catch him?" shouted Penny.

"I'll clip his ear like he did to me," said Aaron, "but he won't get up after I've finished with him."

They drove on in silence until they came to the place where Taneka had lost his Troganbug.

"What's that sticking up?" shouted John, slowing down considerably.

When they were only a few yards from the protruding rock, they all climbed out to have a closer look.

"We'll have to be careful here," said Aaron, One false move and we'll be over the side into this canyon.

"I think, if we go backwards for about 20 yards and then accelerate pulling this wheel back, we may just make it," said John. "Hello, what's this?"

He bent down to have a closer look and noticed that there was a tin lying in the middle of the road. The name printed on the side excited him tremendously.

"We've got a tin of Antisum folks," said John, proudly holding the can for all to see.

"How did that get there?" asked Jimmy gasping.

"I don't know," replied John, "probably Taneka dropped it when he arrived here. It's ours now and it really is going to come in handy.

The children re-boarded the Troganbug and John reversed as planned. He sat there revving the engine for a few moments and then raced back towards the rock and gently pulled back on the wheel. With triumph, they passed over the rock and levelled out again, some yards further across the rocky bridge.

*T*aneka had broken into a jog for the last few miles of the bridge. The wind had got up now and every now and then he had to bend down to prevent being blown off the very narrow rocky terrain.

With great triumph, he came to the end and stepped onto the main land of Planet Mars again. He was pleased with himself. He only had a few miles to go now before he reached the infamous Olympus Mons, the headquarters of Zelmut and the thunderous reception that he would receive.

Throughout his ordeal, since the loss of the Troganbug, he had laid his hand over the pocket that contained the little red book to prevent it accidentally falling out with the efforts of running.

"I'm not about to lose that at this stage," he said.

*T*aneka was close to his goal when he heard the rushing sound of a Troganbug coming up very close behind him. He stopped and looked round for a few moments and noticed that it was closer than he had thought. In fact it was only about 15 yards away from him. There was little he could do to get out of the way and he quickly whipped his hand round to his belt to grab the tin of Antisum. To his horror, he found that it was missing and realising that he must have dropped it when he had the accident earlier, he tried to outrun the machine. But it was futile. The Troganbug with the children aboard drew alongside him very quickly.

*T*he children had been travelling flat out. They felt that they would never catch up with Taneka because he had such a good start on them. Just as they came to the end of the bridge and were firmly back on land, they saw him. Taneka had been running, However realising that this was serving no purpose he stopped and turned to face them.

"It's all over Taneka," shouted John, pleased that they had caught up with the evil teacher turned Martian. "Put your hands up in the air."

"You silly humans," cried Taneka, breaking into a laugh, "you can't do anything to me. You have no weapons for a start."

"We have all we need," shouted Aaron walking towards Taneka. "Give us the book."

Taneka made a lunge for Aaron but this time, Aaron was ready for him and grabbed Taneka's neck and hit him on the jaw knocking him to the ground. Taneka was up in a flash and grabbed Aaron in an arm lock. Just when it appeared that Taneka would overpower Aaron, John, who was now standing very close to the pair of them, fired a blast of the Antisum at Taneka. The effect was instant and Taneka froze to a block of stone.

"Wow, that's amazing," said Jimmy, prodding the frozen mass to check it out. "He's solid. What are we going to do now?"

"Get the book quickly," shouted John, "we've only got about 30 minutes before he comes to."

Aaron tried to go through Taneka's pockets but found that it was not only Taneka that had frozen but his clothes too. Try as he may, he couldn't do anything to get the book out of the pocket.

"I can feel the book," said Aaron, "but it's impossible to open the flap on his pocket. It's solid."

"Can't we rip it off?" asked Penny, joining the boys.

"No. It's turned to stone," replied Aaron, "unless we've a crowbar, we're sunk. Even then, it may damage the book if we try and force it out."

"There's only one answer," said Jimmy, "he'll have to come with us."

"How?" said Penny, "we've only one of these Troganbug things, there'll be no room for us all."

"Aaron," said John, "give me and Jimmy a hand to lift Taneka onto the sidecar. He should be able to balance on there."

The boys huffed and puffed as they lifted the heavy stone figure of the Martian onto the bike. With two attempts, they managed to satisfy themselves that the body wouldn't fall off.

"Right Penny, you sit behind me," said John, "you two, stand on the front and back on the sidecar."

It took a few minutes but they managed to settle on to the Troganbug with Jimmy on the front, sitting on Taneka while Aaron stood on the rear guard.

"Right, let's go," shouted John, "we've got to try and get back to one of those caves before he wakes up again, which should be in about 20 minutes. Keep an eye on him and hold on, here we go."

With that, John gently went forward for a few moments, giving the two boys the chance to get their balance. After a few moments, he was cruising along at about 50mph.

They soon reached the bridge and John slowed down to negotiate this. By now the wind was buffeting them around and this made steering the Troganbug very difficult.

"Don't forget that rock sticking up," shouted Jimmy, hanging on the vehicle as if his very life depended on it, which it did.

"Yes, I know," said John, "it should be just along here somewhere."

Within a few minutes, John could see the formidable rock sticking out of the bridge. Again, he slowed down and revved the engine. When he was satisfied that he had the right ratio, he spurted forward gently pulling the steering column back as far as it would go. The wind was very strong now and elevation was becoming a problem.

John gritted his teeth as the rock came within striking distance and with a final heave back on the controls, the Troganbug just managed to clear the rock with only inches to spare.

"Wow that was close," mumbled Jimmy, silently saying a prayer.

By now, the wind had stirred up a massive dust storm and the children were having to squeeze their eyes together as tight as they could to avoid the stinging grit type stuff that was hitting them in the face. John estimated that they were about 2 miles from the main land and was battling with the ferocious winds that were threatening to blow them into the canyon.

When they were about a mile from their destination, flashes and screams started zooming over their heads.

"It's the Termans," shouted John, choking on the dust that was blowing into his mouth. "They're attacking us."

The children gripped on even more tighter as John accelerated to the machines top speed. Suddenly there was an explosion just in front of them and a massive piece of rock was blown out of the bridge shaking the machine like it was a feather in a high wind.

"It's no good," screamed Penny, ducking as a flash narrowly missed her head, "they're going to hit us."

Just then, John noticed that there were a crowd of the horrible flying creatures standing on the bridge about 20 yards in front of them. To carry on, would have been certain disaster. With lightening skill, he managed to swerve to the right and with panic, the children realised that they were now flying over the canyon with a very long drop below them.

John had noticed through the dust, that there was a set of caves which would be easier to reach than going over the bridge to the caves that they had left earlier.

The Troganbug shot over the vast open space with Termans firing at them with weapons they had not used before. With every bit of power that John could get out of the Troganbug, they eventually hit land and flew straight into a cave with a very wide entrance. John cut the engine bringing the vehicle to a skidding halt narrowly missing the cave wall.

They sat there in silence trying to control their breathing. No one spoke for at least five minutes such was the shock of their little expedition across the dangerous canyon

After a little while, John, whose hands were still gripping the wheel like his very life depended on it, got off the Troganbug and crept to the entrance of the cave.

"Are they out there?" asked Penny, scared out of her wits.

"I can't tell," answered John, "it's very quiet."

"They won't come in here," said Jimmy, "Mr Leonard, I mean that Taneka told us that the Termans never go into the caves."

"Anyway," said Aaron, standing alongside of John, "it's doubtful that they saw where we went, we were travelling so fast."

"I hope you're right," replied John, feeling very worried

"What were those weapons they were using?" asked Aaron, "they were different from the ones that they used on us before."

"Yes," said Penny, "they were exploding all over the place and one nearly took my head off."

"They were using vaporising guns by the sound of it," said Taneka coming round from his stone like appearance.

Thirteen

*J*ohn shot to his feet and ran over to where Taneka was struggling to get off the Troganbug. John had the tin of Antisum poised in his hand as he reached the Martian.

"Hey it's okay," said Taneka. "There's no way that I'm going to try anything while that lot is outside."

"What do you mean?" asked John, staring hard at him.

"Well, they don't know I'm with you," he replied. "They all think that I'm on my way to Olympus Mons to hand in the book to our Chief and Highness, Zelmut."

"Zelmut?" asked Jimmy, "who the flipping heck is that?"

"He is our leader," replied Taneka, "the most feared Martian on the planet. He thinks that I'm on my way to deliver the book to him. That is why the Termans are out there. They're after you. The problem for me is that they'll get me as well."

"Well you're not going to deliver the book to this guy at all," said Aaron, "so give us it now."

"I cannot do that," said Taneka.

"Then we'll throw you outside," said Aaron, getting closer to him. "Then we'll see how long you last."

"That is stupid, human," replied Taneka, "you need me more than you think. I can get you out of here."

"We wouldn't trust you at all," said Penny, "not after you betrayed us."

"Then we will all have a painful time," Taneka went on, "the Termans are out there but they will never come in the caves, However, the warriors will and they'll be here shortly, you can depend on it. Then of course, there is the Blattidae."

"The what?" asked John.

"The Blattidae," repeated Taneka. "It is a large cockroach bigger than you've ever seen. It is bigger that the largest lorry you've ever clapped your eyes on and it is lethal. It'll stop at nothing and will eat anything in its sight. It is the most awesome creature that the Solar system has ever known. The only way to stop this creature is to hit it 3 times with a vaporising gun, right between the eyes. I have never known anyone to be successful in overcoming this creature."

The children all shuddered at the thought of this creature coming near them. John was just going to ask some more questions when there was an almighty explosion just outside of the cave. The force of it made the ground shudder and dust rose in thick clouds from the impact.

"What was that?" shouted Aaron, running to the entrance. He had just got there when a Terman whizzed by his head, almost shooting him with a vaporising gun. Aaron shot backwards and knelt on the ground. It went quiet for a second or two and he looked quickly out of the entrance to try and see how many Termans were out there.

Just then, three Termans flew by close together, again firing at Aaron, narrowly missing him. One of them was unlucky and smashed into the cave wall about three feet from where Aaron was kneeling. Aaron, in an instance, had his first look at a Terman. It was about four foot long with a face like a bat and had very thin legs and huge wings. Its arms and hands though, resembled a human's and this was how it held the vaporising and Antisum guns.

Aaron quickly noticed that the dead Terman had dropped its gun nearby. He quickly made a grab for it and shot back into the cave just missing another dive from two of the Termans.

"Wow, that was close," he said to the others, "but look what I've got," showing them the gun.

The gun resembled a sub-machine gun. It was black in colour with a large yellow dome like contraption on the end of it.

"What type of gun is that?" asked John.

"That, my human friend is a vaporising gun," said Taneka. The yellow dome holds the vaporising agent and is launched when the trigger is pulled.

"Wow, that's brilliant," said Jimmy, "we've got something to fight with now."

"We'll need more than that," said John, crawling to the mouth of the cave.

Just then, there was another loud bang outside of the cave. This time, John saw that there were a small group of ugly things, just like Taneka, coming towards the cave entrance.

"Quick," shouted John in panic, "I think the warriors have turned up."

Without having the chance to familiarise himself with the vaporising gun, Aaron ran forward and fired a quick burst that melted three of the warriors almost instantly.

"Flipping heck," shouted John in excitement. "You're a fantastic shot. Did you see how they melted?"

"Quick, hold this," shouted Aaron, and raced outside the cave to retrieve the guns that had been scattered on the red dusty ground. He was back in a second, but not before a blast from a Terman, splattered into his back. Instantly, he turned to stone.

"Aaron," shouted John, trying to help him. Unfortunately, Aaron had solidified and stood where he had entered the cave, like an Olympic statue.

"Oh that's great," laughed Taneka, running forward to get a better view "that's the best thing I've seen today."

"Shut up you traitor," shouted Jimmy, who was so angry that he took a lunge at Taneka pushing him out into the openness of Planet Mars.

As the others watched this happening, Taneka tried to turn back to the safety of the cave. Unfortunately, he was unlucky and a warrior shot him squarely in the stomach. He vaporised within seconds.

"Well that was good," shouted John, "Taneka's gone but so has the book. We have no chance of returning home now."

The shock of this was quickly forgotten for the moment, as a mighty blast caused a great rock fall near the entrance. Rock after rock began tumbling down so that they were almost cut off. There was just a little light shining through as tons of rock blocked them in.

Thinking on his feet, John commanded that they pick up the solidified statue of Aaron and get on the Troganbug.

"Where are we going?" asked Penny, as John revved the engine.

"We're going to check out this cave," said John. "At the moment, the warriors can't get to us, but it won't take them long to haul the rocks out of the way and rush in."

*T*he cave was dark, damp and bleak as the children made their way through to try and find a way of escape. John's thoughts were all over the place. One part of his mind was focusing on the awful Termans and warriors that were back at the entrance. The other side of his mind was extremely concerned because he had no idea if they would ever be able to get back to the sanity of Planet Earth.

What he would give now to be in one of Mr Jackson's lessons, even if he had to write a 3000 word essay about Thomas Hardy. He would also elect to clean his dad's car or clean the toilet. In fact, he decided that he would do anything, to be able to breathe the peaceful air of his beloved home.

John was so lost in his thoughts that he failed to see the crack of light that shone forth before them. He had been so used to staring at the dim headlights of the Troganbug and listening to his mind turning over and over that it took a loud shout from Jimmy to bring him to a halt.

"John, stop quickly," shouted Jimmy, "look, I can see stars out there."

"John pulled the Troganbug to a halt and stared in the direction that Jimmy was pointing. Sure enough, the stars were shining and the large gap just 20 yards away, looked extremely inviting.

John drove up to the large gap and was completely astounded when he saw that they were on the other side of the canyon again. The cave must have been on the edge of this deep canyon and for miles ahead, there was nothing but a wide open, rocky surface. The intimidating view of Olympus Mons stood in the distance casting a dark shadow over the surrounding area.

Wow, that's amazing," said John, "but we've got to find a place that is safe to hide. The warriors and the Termans will be here soon. Now where can we hide?"

Just like magic, the Troganbug started to drive to the left of the rocky mountain that they had just come out of. After about 100 yards, they came to another series of caves. These were much smaller. John stared at them and made a decision.

"Let's go for that one," he said, pointing to a hole about 6 feet tall by 4 feet wide. "That looks perfect."

John guided the Troganbug through the small entrance of the cave which was just wide enough for the vehicle to get through. The roof, from what they could tell, was only about 8 feet high, but the cave was quite roomy and went back for about 30 feet in all directions.

"This will do," said John, "Now there are some old bushes lying about out there. If we quickly get a large one and plant one in the dust in front of the entrance here, we may just be able to conceal this place.

Jimmy and John went outside and quickly found what they were looking for. Within a few moments, the entrance was well and truly hidden from view and, he hoped, from the warriors that were sure to come looking for them

"Right let's quickly get some ice and some of those Rogangoes and then unload Aaron. Hopefully, he should be coming around in a little while. If we're lucky, our enemy will think we've gone over towards the Olympus Mons and not find this place"

"It's a shame that Aaron can't stay that way," joked Jimmy, "he looks better in stone."

"Oh stop being awful Jimmy," Penny said, "we wouldn't have made it if it hadn't have been for him."

"That's true," said John, looking at the stone face of Aaron with concern."

"I suppose you're right," said Jimmy, trying to cover up his unkind comment.

Fourteen

*T*he children ate their meal of Rogangoes and ice, surprised how hungry they were. They had just finished when Aaron began to come round.

"Wow, what happened?" he asked. "I feel awful and the pain in my back is tremendous."

"Yea an Antisum gun got you mate," said Jimmy, "but you're going to be all right."

"Where's Taneka?" he asked, becoming tense at the sound of the name.

"He's history," said Penny, "Jimmy pushed him outside just after you got shot and he got hit by a vaporising gun."

"Yes," said John, "he just melted before our eyes."

"Amazing," said Jimmy, feeling pleased with himself.

"He'll come back though won't he?" asked Aaron, "he said he was immortal."

"I hope not," said John. "The problem is, he had the book with him. If he doesn't come back to life, we're sunk. We'll never get back home."

*T*hey all sat in silence pondering what John had just said. None of them wanted to admit that the situation was hopeless. They desperately needed something to keep their confidence going.

"Something will turn up," said Aaron, "try not to worry."

"Does your back hurt very much?" asked Penny, feeling quite tender towards him for no apparent reason.

"It's murder," he replied.

"Take your shirt off," said Penny, "and I'll rub some ice on it. It may help."

Aaron did what she asked and within a few moments, he began to feel a little easier.

"Is that better?" she asked him.

"Yes, it's just freezing that's all."

"Well of course it is," said Jimmy, "it's flipping ice it's bound to be cold. By the way, what was it like to be turned to stone?"

"I can't remember anything except running back to the cave," replied Aaron. "It all went very dark then and that was it until I woke up."

*T*he children drifted off into their own thoughts again while Aaron tucked into his meal of ice and Rogangoes. Up to now, they had not heard any more from the warriors or the Termans. In fact, it was very quiet out there and they didn't know if that was a good sign or not.

They all hoped that Taneka would return from the dead. Not that they cared for him but it was the only way they could see of returning back to Planet Earth. However, they had to admit that the chances were very slim.

"Where do you come from Aaron?" asked Penny. "I mean do your parents live near to us or the school?"

"I haven't seen my parents for a year," he replied.

"Why not?" asked John quite shocked at his reply.

"They separated about 18 months ago," he continued." They were always arguing. It was awful. Eventually, dad just left home without even saying goodbye to us. Mum tried to manage but she kept drinking and eventually Social Services put me in care. I've seen them once since then and that was a year ago."

"How awful," said Penny, warming to Aaron more and more.

"That's why I feel so angry all the time," he said. "It's not fair. We had a nice house and all that and then they, threw it all away. It made me feel jealous about every kid I saw from thereon. I just wanted to hurt everyone.

"Yea, we noticed," said John.

"Hmm, I'm sorry about that you guys," Aaron said, "I must have been horrible to you, in fact, I know I was."

"Well we're sorry that we wished that your hair would turn white," said John, "it was wrong of us."

"Well let's start again," said Aaron, "and be friends."

   They all gripped each other's hands, demonstrating their apologies and allegiance to each other and this resulted in quite an emotional few minutes, with the boys trying their best to hide their tears from each other.

"What's your football team?" asked Jimmy.

"Chelsea of course," replied Aaron.

"Oh flipping heck," said John, "we're both Man Utd."

"I'm sure we can put up with that," said Penny laughing until the others saw the funny side too and joined in.

"*I*'m getting concerned about Taneka," said Zelmut to Yermin. "He should have been here long ago. I feel that something may have happened to him.

"He requested the warriors and the Termans," said Yermin, "I hope that he didn't get in the way of their gunfire."

"I'm beginning to think that he did." said Zelmut. "He is, or was a good warrior and would have been here now. I hate to say it but he may have got in the way of the vaporisers."

"If he did, there is nothing we can do," replied Yermin. "he will have been exterminated."

"It is time to send in Blattidae," said Zelmut, "the humans must still be out there so they must be totally destroyed."

"What about the little red book?" asked Yermin. "Taneka must have had that on him when he last made contact. It has either been destroyed along with him or it has fallen into the hand of the humans'"

"I don't think the humans have it," said Zelmut. "If they had, they would be using its power and the Leoxostone would have picked that up, which it hasn't. No I'm afraid, this is a sad day. It looks like I will not receive the power and honour that I richly deserve. Let the Blattidae fulfil my vengeance on the humans. I want them to suffer for this miscarriage of justice."

*B*lattidae was the most awesome and feared creature on the whole of Planet Mars. It was the largest cockroach that the world has ever known, bigger and taller than human or Martian could imagine and it stopped at nothing to crush and eat its prey. Blattidae had the power to outrun any Martian or human and could even overtake a Troganbug at full speed. Martian history showed that no one had ever been able to contend with the skill and determination that the Blattidae displayed.

The warriors dutifully unlocked the large steel gates that had imprisoned Blattidae for many months. They carefully slid the lock out of its place, taking care not to open the doors. With this task completed, they retreated very quickly to the safety of the Headquarters within the awesome Olympus Mons and waited.

From the safety of his empire, Zelmut watched as the doors were smashed open and the angry creature made his escape, racing over the vast open space like he had no time to spare.

"I pity them," Zelmut thought as he stared after the departing Blattidae.

Fifteen

"*B*e quiet," whispered John, hearing a noise outside.

The children held their breath as John crawled to the small cave entrance to see if he could tell what was outside. His stomach churned as he saw at least a dozen warriors walking by, obviously checking to see if the humans were hiding near the rocks.

His heart was pounding and he almost prayed for the first time in his life, as one of the warriors walked towards where he was crouching. The scaly, grey face of the warrior was about five feet from where he was hidden and for one moment, John felt that they would be caught. The warrior was prodding the rocks and moving the branches of their temporary bush when one of the others called him back. Without going any further towards the cave, and obviously not seeing what lay behind the bush, the warrior turned round and went over to the others. After a short conversation, they mounted their Troganbugs and sped off at such a pace that the dust rose to a height of around eight feet, making it impossible to see for quite a while.

"Boy, that was close," said John to the others. "I could almost see the Martian's eyes, he was so close."

"Where are they now?"" asked Aaron walking over to John.

"I haven't a clue," John replied. "One minute they were there and then they raced off almost in a panic. I don't know what that was about."

The children remained inside their quiet little hideout for at least another 30 minutes before they dared to venture out to get a better look at their situation. When they did, they found a very pleasant day with the sun beaming down on their backs as they made their way across the dusty surface towards the large canyon that was nearby.

"It all seems quiet," said Penny.

"Yea, too quiet," said John. "it doesn't seem real. There's something wrong."

"Like what?" asked Penny, becoming a little frightened.

"It's almost like something is waiting to happen." said Aaron rather cautiously. What are we going to do John?"

"I don't know," he replied. "We could stay here but that would serve no purpose. But if we go anywhere, where shall we go? It all seems pointless without the chance of getting the book back."

"I know what you mean," said Jimmy.

"We've got to do something," said Penny anxiously.

"What's that?" asked John pointing to the distance. "There's a great mound of dust but it doesn't look like a storm."

They continued to stare in the direction of where John had been pointing unable to identify what the approaching cloud of dust was. Just then they knew.

"Oh no, look," shouted Aaron, "it's that cockroach thing that Taneka was on about."

"Flipping heck," said Jimmy terrified, "just look at the size of it."

"It's gaining fast as well," shouted John, "quick, get back inside the cave, there's nowhere else we can go. It's travelling at top speed."

The children just managed to get inside the safety of the cave before the hideous creature arrived at the entrance.

"It's outside," screamed Penny, "we're going to be killed."

"Calm down Penny," said Aaron gently patting her on the shoulder, "it can't get in here. We're safe."

Just then, a great length of its antennae crawled into the cave entrance wiping the floor of the cave looking for its prey. Penny just broke into screaming fits as the boys did all they could to prevent the lethal object from scooping them out. The antennae overall was about thirty feet in length and the thickness of a drainpipe with hairy tentacles all over it.

The probing of this awesome object continued and the children were running out of space to run to in order to avoid the impact. The result of this would have meant being dragged out into the waiting jaws of this horrible creature. All of the time, the Blattidae made loud rasping noises that grated through the children's nerves

Just then, Aaron picked up a huge rock and smashed it down on the tip of the antennae. The roar from the Blattidae was deafening and it retreated into the open giving the children some well-earned respite.

"Quick," shouted John, running to the Troganbug, "this is our only chance. Jump on. We'll try and blast our way out."

"No," screamed Penny, "we'll be killed."

Aaron gently helped her to the waiting Troganbug and when they were all settled on it, John revved the engine with a piercing velocity. Within seconds, the Troganbug had shot out of the tiny entrance completely taking the Blattidae by surprise.

John steered the vehicle towards the open canyon. The surprise of the Blattidae was only temporary and within moments he began chasing them across the uneven surface of the Planet.

"Quickly, he's gaining on us," shouted Aaron, terrified of the horrible beast.

While John went at a tremendous speed, Aaron and Jimmy tried to hit the beast with the Vaporising guns. However, the Troganbug was lurching around so much that they found it difficult to make any shot count.

They were now about a hundred yards from the very deep canyon. The Blattidae was only about fifteen yards behind them and was gaining fast. Aaron crouched as low as he could and took a careful aim and shot the vaporising gun again. This time, he was successful and the shot hit the beast right between the eyes.

"Got him," shouted Aaron in triumph as the Blattidae pulled up sharply, obviously in great pain. "We've only got to get two more to kill it."

However, the shot only angered the beast even more and he began gaining on them again. John, by now was at the edge of the canyon. He had chosen to come this way because he guessed that the creature would not be able to fly. It would mean driving off the main land and hovering in space but that was better than ending up in the jaws of this ferocious beast.

"Hold on tight," John shouted, "we're going airborne."

They all screamed as the Troganbug left the land and shot into the open space of the deep canyon. The beast who was only a few yards behind them, came to a screeching halt yards from the canyon edge. With frustration, it let out a long, rasping roar that made the children's hair stand up on their bodies.

John slowed the Troganbug to about forty mph, the lowest speed he dare go down to. He went round and round in great circles trying to contemplate what the great beast was going to do next. Just then, the Troganbug began to shake and splutter and began to lose altitude. John remained calm, even though his heart was racing and he managed to correct the machine.

"What's happening?" shouted Jimmy in panic, frantically hanging on to the Troganbug in order to prevent himself falling off.

"I don't know," shouted John, "but, we're going to have to get back on the land I'm afraid because I have a funny feeling that something is seriously wrong with this thing."

John managed to get the Troganbug to the right altitude and just managed to land on the main land again with a series of splutters from the engine. The Blattidae wasted no time at all and began to race over to where they had landed, about one hundred and fifty yards away.

Just when the children had given up all hope of being able to fight this creature there appeared the most amazing sight the children had ever seen. The Blattidae, also spotting the awesome sight, pulled up sharply and roared. The children stared in disbelief at the figure of something like a man with a large sword in his hands. The figure was at least thirty feet high, tall and proud and was totally gold all over. The figure, in fact, was so bright that it actually hurt the children's eyes to stare at it for too long. This was also evident of the creature because it kept blinking.

The Blattidae made a lunge at the golden figure of a man but it was no match for his strength. The figure struck the Blattidae around the throat with his sword and the creature screamed in agony. Again the man lunged at the creature, hacking it across the antennae area and completely disabling it. With one mighty lunge, the sword was thrust in between the eyes of the creature and it collapsed in a heap in the dust. The fight was over and the creature lay dead.

The figure of the man, turned towards the children and as he walked towards them, he shrunk in size until he was about six feet tall. He was still very bright and as he came up close to them, the children found it impossible to fix their gaze upon him.

The children were surprised that they were not afraid of him, in fact, they felt immense peace as he stood before them and spoke.

"The battle is over my dear ones," he said to them "There is nothing more to fear. You have been honourable in your management of the little red book which I have here."

The golden figure of the man handed the book to John and smiled at him with the most beautiful eyes that John had ever seen. His words were warm and kind and the most amazing peace fell upon them all.

"You have passed the test. You could have wished for anything you wanted and it would have been granted. Instead, you showed a selfless attitude that has warmed my heart. Go now in peace and take this book back to its rightful owner, Pedro Armaz. You will not have to wish to get there. I am sending you. Go in peace and you will surely be blessed and made prosperous."

With that, the children heard the same hissing sound and then came the beautiful colours as they were transported back to Planet Earth.

Sixteen

Tenerife is a very hot place practically all the year around. Perhaps the hottest month could well be August when the temperature can rise to around 46C, which is hot.

Also one of the most beautiful and awesome sights is the sea at sunset. Viewed from the wide path that runs from Playa de las Americas to Los Christianos, the eye takes in the lovely palm trees and looks out to the horizon that just before sunset, has a giant shadow cast upon it. This appears to be a mountain range coming out of the sea but is in fact the shadow that is cast upon it from Mount Teide.

This was the view that John, Penny, Jimmy and Aaron were looking at as they found themselves sitting on the beach at Los Christianos. It was about 8.45pm on a warm August evening when they realised where they were. People could be seen for miles as they walked to and fro along the long walkway. However, whereas the people were either residents or holiday makers, the children were here on an assignment – to deliver the little red book to Pedro Armaz.

The children had asked traders about the whereabouts of the Armaz family and it seemed that everyone they asked knew them. Therefore they now were on the beach just in front of the Armaz home.

"I feel quite scared," said John.

"What, after all we've been through?" said Penny, "this should be a doddle compared to that."

"Yes, too true," said Aaron.

"Are we going to see him then?" said Jimmy. "I want to go home."

The children all shared Jimmy's sentiments and were eager to complete this mission. They also didn't know what sort of a reception they would get when they met this man. Somehow, he didn't seem like a stranger. In fact, they felt they had known him for years, so much had happened to them through his book.

"Come on then," said John, "let's get it over with."

The children walked up the slope to the little walkway and into the gate that led the way to the Armaz villa. It was a beautiful, spacious white bungalow, with an orange roof that could be seen for miles. The property was set on a hill that meant the children had a little climb before they reached the main door.

The gardens were lovely with large palm trees, cactus, geraniums and other colourful flowers that gave off the most amazing scent that lingered in their nostrils. In the corner of the garden opposite the door, sat an elderly gentleman in a panama hat.

"Hello children," he said gently in a combination of English and Spanish. "I have a feeling I know why you have come to see me. You have my little red book, I believe."

"How did you know?" asked John, amazed.

"I felt it in my spirit," he replied, "come into the house."

Pedro Armaz shuffled across the garden and climbed the step into this beautiful villa. He led them into the kitchen and offered them a seat at the table. The children sat down and began to tell him how they had come across the book and everything that had happened to them since then.

At the end of their discourse, Pedro Armaz sat back in the wooden chair and had tears in his eyes. He was silent for a moment or two while he gathered together his emotions. After a second or two, he began to speak to them.

""You have no idea what this means to me," he began. "I received the words for this book when I was a child and my parents were working all the hours of the day to give us what they could. Our lives changed for the better and I made a vow that this book would be handed down from generation to generation. When it was stolen, I thought that would never happen. Now, it is a dream that has come true. An answer to my many prayers and I have you to thank for this.

"We didn't do anything," said John, "in fact, instead of returning it to you when we found it, we decided to use it to enjoy ourselves."

"But you were never greedy," he replied, "and now you have a wish that will be granted. In fact, you will be transported home in a few moments and you and your families will be made prosperous and have peace in your lives."

The conversation was over and Pedro made them stand up. There was a flash of many colours and then came the rushing sound and within moments, the children were sitting in John's room as if nothing had happened.

"Has this really happened?" asked John, "I feel that it was a dream, I just can't believe it."

"Yes, me too," said Jimmy.

"Perhaps it was a dream," said Aaron.

"No it was too vivid," replied Penny. "Too much has happened."

Just then, John's father shouted up the stairs that their dinner was ready.

"We'll have to go," said John, "we'll have to face the flack of where we've been I suppose. Hold on, though, how did dad know we were up here, haven't we been missing for days?"

The children decided to go down and face their parents and then to meet up later in the evening, if they were allowed out. They let Jimmy and Aaron out and went into the kitchen.

"Did you have a good day at school," John's mum asked. "We've hardly seen you since you came home."

"It was a dream," thought Penny as John answered that school had been fine.

"This is weird," whispered John to Penny as their parents served the dinner up. "It must have been a dream. We just didn't go to Planet Mars."

Just then, John feeling something in his pocket drew out a Rogangoes that he must have left there earlier. The twins just looked at each other in amazement.

*L*ater that night, the Friday night that they had gone to Planet Mars, the children got together and each shared similar stories.

"It's amazing," said Jimmy. "It's still Friday and yet it seems we've been away for about a week or so."

"We have," said Aaron, "but somehow, time must have stood still, like we were in a type of time lapse. It's awesome."

"Well at least Mr Armaz was happy," said Penny, "his face was amazing when John gave him the book."

*T*he following night, John, Penny and the others had decided to have a night at home. The twins were upstairs when they heard their father give a loud shout and their parents started shouting for joy.

"What's going on," said John, running down the stairs with Penny on his tail.

"We're rich," shouted Mr Carter as they went into the lounge. We've just won a part of the Lottery."

"How much?" asked Penny, astounded.

"A million pounds," cried their mum, jumping for joy

"Our ship has come in at last," shouted their dad, hardly able to contain himself. "We'll be able to buy that house down the road that we've been looking at and I'm going to start my own business. Do you fancy a new laptop each?"

The children could hardly contain their excitement and joined in the celebrations with their parents.

Later, when they were upstairs, John's mobile rang.

"John," Aaron's voice said, "my parents are getting back together. Dad's been promoted in his job and he's bought a new house. Isn't that fantastic? I must go now, I'll see you tomorrow."

John hardly had the chance to tell Penny, when the doorbell rang.

"Jimmy's here to see you kids," shouted their dad.

A second later, Jimmy rushed into John's bedroom where John and Penny were.

"Guess what?" Jimmy said excited. "You know how my dad's been writing books for years. Well, he's had one accepted for publication and he's been paid a whopping advance. They're going to buy a new house."

John and Penny found it very difficult to make sense of all that had happened in such a short space of time. They eagerly shared theirs and Aaron's news with Jimmy and they all hugged themselves, jumping around in a circle for ages.

In the end, they had to agree to leave everything until the morning. They were all so excited that they were becoming euphoric.

The head teacher went into his garage to find a screwdriver to fix a fuse. He was astonished as he switched on the light and stared at his car. It was the colour green that he had first chosen when he purchased it.

EPILOGUE

"Was that God we saw do you think, or an Angel?" Jimmy asked.

"I don't know," said Aaron, "but he had the most amazing voice."

"Yes," said Penny, "and he filled me with so much peace that I wanted to cry."

"He was an amazing fighter," said John, "look what he did to that cockroach thing."

"The Blattidae," said Jimmy. "Yea, that was great."

"I think it was God," said John, "I mean, he had the book when it had obviously been destroyed and he got us back here without even wishing."

"Yes, and the way he spoke to us," said Aaron, "and the things that have happened to our families since. It just had to be God."

"Wow," was all Penny could say.

"Well, I know one thing," said Jimmy, "I think I'll go to church on Sunday,"

"Yes," me too," said the others together.

Meanwhile, Zelmut was furious.

"The Almighty has won this battle and stolen my power, but I'll get it back. I want that book! Bring me Pedro Armaz and those human children."

Find out what happens to Pedro Armaz

and the children in Grahame Howard's

next novel

The Wishing Book 2 – Return to Mars